HORSE

DISCARD

Horsemen of Terror

LEFT BEHIND
>THE KIDS<

Jerry B. Jenkins
Tim LaHaye

WITH CHRIS FABRY

TYNDALE HOUSE PUBLISHERS, INC.
WHEATON, ILLINOIS

Visit Tyndale's exciting Web site at www.tyndale.com

Discover the latest Left Behind news at www.leftbehind.com

Published in association with the literary agency of Alive Communications, Inc., 7680 Goddard Street, Suite 200, Colorado Springs, CO 80920.

Edited by Curtis H. C. Lundgren

ISBN 0-8423-4317-2, mass paper

Printed in the United States of America

08 07 06 05 04 03 02
9   8   7   6   5   4   3   2   1

To Kelli, Alyssa, Jesse, and Tyler Middleton

TABLE OF CONTENTS

What's Gone On Before

JUDD Thompson Jr. and the rest of the Young Tribulation Force are involved in the adventure of a lifetime. After fleeing New Babylon, Judd helps his friends Nada and Kasim unite with their family in Israel. Judd is overjoyed to see the return of Mr. Stein, who tells amazing stories of miracles God has performed in Africa.

Vicki Byrne and her friends escape a Global Community trap in Johnson City, Tennessee, and return to Illinois. Though they know it's risky, the kids turn the schoolhouse into a hospital for people suffering from locust stings. As believers around the country hear about Vicki's teaching from the kids' Web site, groups ask her to visit. Finally, Vicki agrees and sets out on a cross-country trip with Conrad and Shelly.

Judd worries about Nada when he doesn't hear from her. When their friend Sam Goldberg returns from being questioned by the Global Community, Sam tells them Nada and her family are being held in a GC jail.

Vicki can't believe the success of the cross-country trip. Believers are inspired by her message while many others receive the mark of the true believer. In Arizona, Vicki mentions the story of Buck Williams and is approached afterward by a middle-aged man. "I want to thank you for coming and talking. I was especially interested in the journalist you talked about."

"Mr. Williams has a great story," Vicki said.

"Yeah, I've heard it before. Too much, as a matter of fact."

Vicki folded her arms. "What do you mean?"

"My name is Jeff Williams. Buck is my brother."

Follow the Young Tribulation Force as they try to make the most of every opportunity to tell others about God before the next terrible judgment.

ONE

Jeff Williams

VICKI Byrne stared at the man. She couldn't believe he was actually Buck Williams's brother.

"I live with my dad not far from here," Jeff said. "We've tried to keep the business going, but it's been tough."

"Business?"

"Dad owns a trucking company. We bring fuel into the state, mostly from Oklahoma and Texas. At least we used to. With everything that's happened, we're just scraping by."

Jeff explained that he had worked his way up in the family business and now handled the day-to-day operations. "Dad always thought Buck would come back and help us out, but he went away to school and we haven't seen much of him since. He wasn't here when Mom died. . . ."

As others left the house, Jeff moved toward

the door. "Better get back. Nice talking to you."

"Wait," Vicki said. "You must have come here for a reason."

"I heard about this church from a guy. This is only my second time."

"Do you have any other family?"

Jeff looked away and took a deep breath. "A wife and two children. They're gone."

"I'm so sorry," Vicki said.

"My wife was picking up our kids at a retreat in the mountains. There was an accident. Her car flipped. The state police never found her body, just her clothes."

"The night of the disappearances?"

Jeff nodded. "They found a late-night snack burning on the stove and a hundred sets of pajamas, but my kids were gone. I took the four-wheel drive up there to see for myself. Then I went to the cabin where all those kids were."

Jeff sat and put his face in his hands. "Thought I was over this. I told Dad I was finally moving on, but hearing you brought it all back."

"What was your wife like?" Vicki said.

"Sharon and I had our problems before the kids came along. We even split up for a while but got back together after she got religion. She really changed. Losing her and the kids has been the hardest thing I've ever gone through."

"Have you talked to the pastor here about this?"

Jeff glanced at the man. "Dad would have a fit if he knew I was here. He doesn't agree with Buck that we're not Christians."

"What do you think?"

Jeff looked away.

"Your wife and children didn't die that night," Vicki said.

"Buck talked to my dad and told us his theory."

"It's not a theory. The Bible is coming true all around us every day. . . ."

"At first I thought this whole thing was like the last judgment of God. But if he took all the good people and left the bad ones, why were my dad and me left behind? What did we do to deserve this? Earthquakes, meteors, and stinging bugs. This can't be from God."

"God cares about you, Jeff. He gave his life for you, and now you've been given a second chance to follow him."

Jeff scowled. "Promise me something."

"What?"

"Don't ever tell Buck or anybody else that you saw me here."

Vicki glanced at Conrad and Shelly, who

seemed to be listening. "We won't. But we'll be here another couple of days. There are answers that you and your father should hear."

Jeff shook his head and walked toward the door. He turned and said, "Leave my dad out of this."

Conrad, Shelly, and the pastor joined Vicki. The pastor said he had seen Jeff only once before. "I tried to talk with him myself, but he slipped out before I had the chance."

"Buck has tried to get through to him, hasn't he?" Conrad said.

"Sounds like they haven't had a very good relationship," Vicki said.

"Maybe we should try to find him and his dad," Shelly said.

The pastor shook his head. "I don't want to scare him away. Let's pray and ask God to work on him."

Judd listened as Sam told more about being questioned by the Global Community. Sam didn't know for sure why he had been released, but he thought his father might have been involved. Plus, he had spoken so much about God that many prisoners had believed in Jesus. The most troubling part of Sam's story was that Nada and her family had been taken into custody. Judd and Lionel pulled Sam aside and asked to hear the whole story.

"The guards brought Kasim and Jamal inside and treated them roughly," Sam said. "Kasim got the worst of it. They put them in separate cells so they wouldn't be able to talk. Kasim was near me."

"Did Kasim talk with you?" Judd said.

Sam nodded. "Kasim wanted to be careful. His lip was bloody and he was in a lot of pain. But he whispered that the GC came a few nights ago. Kasim and Nada slipped out a window and thought they had gotten away, but a squad car cornered them in an alley."

"How could the GC have found them?" Lionel said.

"Kweesa," Judd said.

Sam nodded again. "Kasim told me about calling his old girlfriend in New Babylon. He was sure she was the one who gave his family away. They probably traced Kasim's call."

"Then the GC know who he is," Judd said.

"Kasim thinks they'll try him as a deserter," Sam said. "And you can bet the deputy commander recognized Jamal and the rest of the family as soon as he saw them."

Judd put a hand to his forehead. "You're

right. Woodruff was questioning them in the apartment when he got stung. He'll fry them."

"We have to get them out," Sam said. "Our only chance is my dad. We should pray for him to believe the truth and then somehow release them."

"There might be another way," Judd said.

※

Mark Eisman tried calling Vicki throughout the day but didn't connect until late evening. Vicki said the trip to Arizona had been interesting, but she wouldn't go into detail.

"A lot's been happening here too," Mark said. "Have you heard the news?"

"What news?"

"They're starting up school again."

"What school?"

"The Global Community Department of Education made a statement today. They're setting up satellite schools around the country. I just heard a couple days ago about the final decision."

"Let me guess," Vicki said. "Carl found out about it in Florida."

"Bingo," Mark said. "He was going through some top secret GC files and found a memo from the GC's top guy in education, Dr. Neal

Damosa. He's handpicked by Carpathia for the United North American States."

"What did the memo say?"

"They've been planning this for a long time, but with each judgment, they've had to put it off."

"Put what off?"

"Requiring everyone under the age of twenty to go through what they're calling continuing education."

"Brainwashing," Vicki said.

"Exactly," Mark said. "There are thousands of sites across the U.S. where they'll register kids and have them go through training beamed by satellite."

"What are they going to teach?"

Mark pulled up the memo on his computer screen and read parts to Vicki. *"We exist to make our students better members of the Global Community. We will teach tolerance and the ideals represented by our leader, Potentate Nicolae Carpathia.*

"Our hope is to also identify those who might be candidates for our Morale Monitor squad. Each location will be asked to screen students for this elite team of committed young people."

Vicki sighed. "I had hoped after Commander Blancka that the Morale Monitors would end."

"It gets worse," Mark said. "Listen. *Not only will we identify those loyal to our cause, but we will also target those against our goals. Some would like to see the downfall of the Global Community. No doubt they have been brainwashed by parents, friends, or heretics such as Tsion Ben-Judah. Young people who refuse to attend our learning facilities will be rounded up and processed.*"

"Processed?" Vicki said. "Like we're slabs of meat."

"They mean business," Mark said. "We showed the announcement to everybody here today, and a bunch of unbelievers left."

"Melinda and Janie?"

"No. Janie's worried about getting sent back to prison. Melinda says she's waiting until you get back before she decides what to do."

"Then we have to come home right away," Vicki said.

"You have more meetings."

"We've been gone too long. Cancel our other meetings and tell the groups we'll do our best to reschedule. I need to clear up a couple of things here, and we'll hopefully make it by the end of the week."

"I'll tell Melinda," Mark said.

"One more thing. How close is the nearest GC learning center?"

"A few miles from the town where we found Lenore," Mark said.

"Sounds too close," Vicki said. "If those people who stayed with us rat us out, we're dead. We need a plan in case the GC come looking."

"I'm on it," Mark said.

He hung up and wrote e-mails to the groups who had requested teaching from the Young Tribulation Force. He said he hated letting them down, but he hoped they would understand.

Lenore sat by Mark and looked over his shoulder. "Maybe having all those people stay with us wasn't such a good idea."

Mark kept typing. "We all agreed to take care of them. What we need is a backup plan in case any of them inform the GC about us. Any suggestions?"

※

Judd closed the bedroom door and huddled with Sam and Lionel. He pulled out a sheet of paper and drew a diagram. "They held me in the same jail. I know how the offices and cells are laid out. Sam, you were just there. If we can figure a way in, I think we can get them out."

Lionel shook his head. "We've done enough damage. If the GC catch us . . ."

"Damage?" Judd said. "If it were you in there, Nada would try to get you out."

"That's what's wrong with her. She shouldn't try that kind of thing."

"I'm not leaving her in there!" Judd shouted.

Sam started to speak, but the door opened. Mr. Stein walked in and sat on the bed. "I know what you're thinking, and I don't blame you. I can't imagine what Jamal's family is going through. But I can't let you attempt an escape—"

"We have to get them out," Judd said. "Kasim's life's at stake."

"I know that. Allow me to finish. I can't let you attempt an escape without *my* help."

"You'll help us?" Sam said.

"We must come up with a plan we all agree on," Mr. Stein said. He looked at Judd and Lionel. "That should be no small task."

They laughed, then spread out several sheets of paper on the bed. They worked until early the next morning.

🔆

Vicki looked for Jeff the next day but didn't see him. She sped up the teaching and told the participants that she and her friends had to leave that night. When Vicki opened the floor for questions, kids asked about the start-up of the Global Community satellite schools.

"What should we do?" a girl asked. "They could brainwash us, and we'll lose the mark of the believer. But if we don't go, they'll know we're against the Global Community."

"You don't have to worry about losing the mark." Vicki explained that the kids who believe in Jesus are held not by their own power, but by God's. "Each of you has to make up your own mind. By going you might be able to reach some people who don't know about God. But it might be too much for you to listen to the GC's blather."

"What are you going to do?" another teen said.

Vicki glanced at Conrad and Shelly. "I'd like to ask you all to pray for us as we head back tonight. We have to resolve some issues about the place we're staying and some people we've taken in."

Kids stood and held hands. The pastor led them in a prayer and asked God to protect Vicki and her friends as they traveled. Other kids prayed simple prayers and thanked God for bringing Vicki and the others to help them learn.

As they were praying, the door opened. Vicki looked up and noticed Jeff Williams slip into the back of the room. When they were finished, Vicki walked up to him. "I'm glad you came back."

"What you said makes sense, but I'm not sure I can believe it."

"Why?"

Jeff frowned. "It would mean Buck was right." He sat and leaned back in his chair. Shelly, Conrad, and the pastor joined them. "I'm ticked off at Buck right now. I mean, I'm proud of him and everything. He's accomplished a lot. But he didn't even come to Sharon and the kids' memorial service."

Vicki started to speak, but Jeff held up a hand. "I know he was probably busy with a story or something. I also know I shouldn't base a spiritual decision on what Buck did or didn't do."

The pastor leaned forward. "Jeff, you know the truth now. You were left behind because you didn't have a true relationship with God like your wife did. Give your heart to God right now."

Jeff stood. "I need more time."

"I understand," the pastor said. "But don't wait too long. We don't know how many will make it through the next judgment."

Jeff turned to Vicki. "You promised not to tell my brother or anybody else that you saw me here."

Vicki nodded. She felt bad as she watched Jeff leave. She wanted him to pray right then and bring his father to the church. But she knew no one could make the decision for Jeff. He had to make it himself.

Before they left, the pastor gave the kids some extra food to take on their trip. Since the man's computer had been destroyed in the earthquake, Conrad suggested they let him have theirs. Vicki and Shelly agreed.

Vicki's phone rang. "I just heard from Carl," Mark said. "Are you sitting down?"

"Just tell me."

"Remember the guy who helped you out in Tennessee?"

"Omer?"

"Yeah. He and a bunch of others from Johnson City stormed the GC prison to try and rescue the believers."

"Is he—?"

"The GC killed most of them. Omer's gone, Vick."

Vicki slid to the floor. Shelly knelt beside her and put a hand on her shoulder.

"The worst part is that the GC were getting ready to release Omer's mom. Carl said if they had waited a few more days, everything would have been all right."

TWO

First Sighting

VICKI stretched out in the back of the van and thought of the disaster and death that had become so common. The world had changed on the awful night of the disappearances, but with each passing day things got worse. Losing her parents, sister, and brother was only the start. She had been adopted by Bruce Barnes, the pastor who had helped the kids know God. Bruce had died in a fiery explosion at the start of World War III. Then, Ryan Daley, one of the original members of the Young Trib Force, had been killed during the wrath of the Lamb earthquake.

With each day, Vicki grew numb. She didn't want to. She wanted to feel alive. With each person who prayed and asked God for forgiveness, she felt a spark in her soul. Then something else would happen, like the news of Omer, and she would become preoccupied again. She knew the Bible taught that things would get worse and worse. In four months they would reach the halfway point of the seven-year tribulation. Then would come the Great Tribulation. Vicki trembled. Nicolae Carpathia was bad enough now, but the Great Tribulation would make this seem like a picnic.

She wanted to survive all seven years and see the Glorious Appearing of Christ and his victory over evil. But how? In time, the Global Community would force people to identify with Nicolae or face the consequences. That was something she simply would not do. Rabbi Tsion Ben-Judah believed only one-fourth of the population alive after the Rapture would survive until the end. Would Vicki be among them? And what of her friends? What about Judd?

Vicki prayed for Jeff Williams and his father. She prayed for each group she had met over the past few weeks and asked God to continue raising up house churches around the country. She felt exhausted but kept praying and pleading with God for believers she knew. She thought of Chloe Williams and her new baby. How difficult it must be bringing up a child in a world like this. Chloe had a lot of work to do with the commodity co-op. Now she would need to care for little Kenny. Vicki

prayed that Chloe would have new
strength each day.

Vicki pulled out a flashlight and a printout
the pastor in Arizona had handed her before
they left. It was the latest copy of *The Truth*, a
cyberspace magazine. The articles were written anonymously, but the kids had heard
this was Buck Williams's new writing project.
Buck told the truth about Nicolae Carpathia
and the Global Community. The latest
edition gave more information about the
so-called satellite schools.

The article included photos of locations
ready for students. "These schools will not
teach reading, writing, and arithmetic," Buck
wrote. "Instead, they will soak young people
with Global Community propaganda. We
can only hope the next generation will see
through the smoke and mirrors and find the
truth found in the Bible."

*Buck sure wouldn't have been able to write
that in* Global Community Weekly, Vicki
thought.

The next few pages were printed from
www.theunderground-online.com. Mark had
posted Tsion Ben-Judah's latest Internet
offering.

> *My text is from Revelation 9:15-21. "And
> the four angels who had been prepared for*

this hour and day and month and year were turned loose to kill one-third of all the people on earth. They led an army of 200 million mounted troops—I heard an announcement of how many there were.

"And in my vision, I saw the horses and the riders sitting on them. The riders wore armor that was fiery red and sky blue and yellow. The horses' heads were like the heads of lions, and fire and smoke and burning sulfur billowed from their mouths. One-third of all the people on earth were killed by these three plagues—by the fire and the smoke and burning sulfur that came from the mouths of the horses. Their power was in their mouths, but also in their tails. For their tails had heads like snakes, with the power to injure people.

"But the people who did not die in these plagues still refused to turn from their evil deeds. They continued to worship demons and idols made of gold, silver, bronze, stone, and wood—idols that neither see nor hear nor walk! And they did not repent of their murders or their witchcraft or their immorality or their thefts."

Vicki shivered as she read. She pictured the frightening beasts and riders and the millions who would die.

This passage has puzzled me for some time. For centuries scholars have looked at prophecy as symbolic. These symbols have been explained in different ways by different people. But why would God make it so difficult? I believe when the Scriptures say the writer saw something in a vision, it is symbolic of something else. But when the writer simply says that certain things happen, I take those literally. So far I have been proven right. This passage says John sees 200 million horsemen in a vision. I doubt these men and animals will be flesh and bone since John mentions a vision, but they will have a terrible impact on the world. They will indeed kill a third of the population. Friends, I don't know how this will happen or even how long it will take. God could make it occur in an instant. It appears to me that it will take several weeks. I ask you to read the account in Revelation and ask God to make it clear to you.

Vicki folded the pages and stuffed them in her pocket. She rubbed her eyes and asked Shelly and Conrad if they needed anything.

"Rest," Conrad said.

Vicki awoke in what seemed like a few minutes. She looked at the clock on the dashboard and saw that she had been asleep four hours. Conrad glanced in the rearview mirror.

"Are they still back there?" Shelly said.

"Yeah," Conrad said.

Vicki sat up. "What's wrong?"

"Somebody's following us," Conrad said.

Vicki turned but didn't see any cars. In the moonlight she spotted a mountain range and a butte in the distance. "Where are we?"

"South of Denver," Shelly said. "Mark showed us a highway that should take us straight to Illinois, but—"

Conrad whipped the van to the left as a car parked alongside the road suddenly pulled out in front of them. Shelly screamed and hit her head against the side window. Conrad veered inches from the car and struggled to regain control. He nearly went off the side of the road but managed to get the van back on the pavement.

"They must be working together," Conrad said.

Vicki glanced behind them and saw two sets of headlights. "They're gaining on us."

"Is it the GC?" Shelly said, putting a hand over a knot on her head.

"It might be worse," Conrad said.

Judd and the others considered several plans to help Nada and her family. Judd wanted to create some kind of diversion outside of headquarters. Sam suggested they slip sleeping pills into the station's coffeepot.

Finally, Mr. Stein said he was going to bed. "I think we should all pray about what we're going to do."

Judd shook his head as Mr. Stein left. "How can we sit here and pray when we know they're in trouble?"

Sam put his arms behind his head and stretched. "I understand how you feel. You want to get in there and get them out."

"If we don't, they're toast."

"If we don't come up with something soon, I'll go to my father."

"You can't do that."

Sam sighed. "Part of me wants to run in there with pepper spray and disable the guards. But I still hold out hope that my father will believe. I don't want him to think we're some kind of radical military group. I want him to see Christ in what we do."

The morning sun was coming up as they each fell asleep. Mr. Stein awakened them. "It's time."

"Time for what?" Judd said.

"God has spoken. He revealed that we should go to the station quickly."

"What are we going to do?" Sam said.

"Get dressed. We must go."

※

Vicki watched the two sets of headlights rapidly approach. One set was an old truck. The other was a smaller sports car. "Can't you go faster?"

"There's no way we're going to outrun them!" Shelly screamed.

"We're going uphill," Conrad said. "I'm going to try something."

Conrad jerked the wheel to the right, and the van ran into a ditch and up the side of a gully. Even though she was buckled in, Vicki's head hit the ceiling. Finally, the van reached a dirt riding path that ran parallel to the road.

Vicki glanced behind them. The truck was a few hundred yards behind. The sports car was still on the main road.

"I'm going to try something else," Conrad said. He turned off the headlights, plunging them into darkness. Vicki could barely see the lights of the truck through the dust they had kicked up. The sports car slowed and pulled to the side of the road.

"Maybe they'll think we went off a cliff or something," Conrad said. "Hang on!"

He jerked the van to the right and drove straight through a wooden fence and onto another road. They found an overpass and headed west. Conrad drove wildly across an open field. He slowed as they hit a winding stretch of road. He turned his headlights on for an instant to get his bearings. They crossed railroad tracks and turned into a gravel parking lot. Vicki spotted old playground equipment and a lake. Conrad drove onto a jogging path and parked the van behind an abandoned picnic shelter.

The three got out and kept watch. A few minutes later the sports car flew over the railroad tracks and wound its way around the lake. The truck followed moments later.

"You think we're safe?" Vicki said.

Conrad turned. "Let's get back to the main—" He stopped midsentence and grabbed Shelly by the shoulders. Shelly stared straight ahead, shaking.

"What's wrong, Shel?" Vicki said.

Shelly dropped to her knees and gasped for air. She pointed toward the lake.

Vicki and Conrad looked but didn't see anything. The cars were out of sight now.

"They're gone," Conrad said. "Don't worry."

Shelly trembled, as if she had just walked out of a freezer. She rubbed her arms and shook. Vicki knelt beside her and looked into Shelly's eyes. Total fear.

"I think she's going into shock," Vicki said.

"Get her in the car and let's get out of here."

✳

Judd followed Mr. Stein, Sam, and Lionel through the narrow streets that led to the GC headquarters. Judd asked several times what they were going to do, but Mr. Stein merely shrugged.

When they neared GC headquarters, Mr. Stein took them to a small café across the street. The four sat, and Mr. Stein ordered each of them something to drink. When the waiter left, Mr. Stein scratched his beard. "I have felt such a strong urge to be here, but I don't know why."

"This happened a lot on your trip, didn't it?" Lionel said.

Mr. Stein smiled. "There were many times when I didn't know my next move, but I simply trusted God. This feels the same. I know God wants me to speak about him, but

I have no idea how this could gain the release of your friends."

The kids studied the headquarters building. Sam said, "We don't even know if they're still—"

Sam stopped as the front door to headquarters opened. Deputy Commander Woodruff and Sam's father stepped outside. Woodruff was yelling at Mr. Goldberg.

Mr. Stein turned. "I believe this is it. I have to go."

Judd stood, but Mr. Stein held up a hand. "Please. I have to go alone."

※

Vicki held Shelly in the backseat as Conrad drove back to the main road. Shelly shook violently, and Vicki couldn't calm her.

"I think we're okay now," Conrad said. "We're leaving those guys behind."

"Good," Vicki said. She pushed Shelly's hair from her face. "See, you don't have to worry about those guys."

"I-I-I'm not," Shelly managed. "Th-th-that's not what scared me."

"Then what on earth did?"

"Not what *on* earth, but what was above it."

"What do you mean?"

"You didn't see them? They were hovering

over the water by the mountain. It was the most awful thing I've ever seen." Shelly put her face in her hands.

Vicki glanced at Conrad in the rearview mirror. He shrugged. Vicki turned to Shelly. "What scared you?"

Shelly swallowed hard and closed her eyes. "Horses. Huge horses that looked like lions."

THREE

Bandits

VICKI leaned close to Shelly. "Are you sure you didn't fall asleep and dream about it?"

"They were there, I swear. Just as real as you and me."

"We believe you," Conrad said. "We just didn't see anything."

"You said they were above the ground?" Vicki said.

Shelly nodded. "It was like they were walking on air. And they were huge."

Vicki felt confused. Tsion had written that the horses would be some kind of angelic beings, unseen to the human eye. If Shelly had seen them, they were real and the next judgment was about to begin.

Conrad hit the accelerator. Vicki turned and saw the same car and truck. "These guys don't give up."

The truck pulled along their right side, and the car raced on their left. The driver of the truck wore a hat and had a stubbly beard. He pointed and yelled.

"Whatever you do, don't stop!" Vicki said.

A woman rode in the passenger seat of the sports car. She rolled down her window and yelled, "Pull over!" When Conrad didn't obey, she turned to the driver.

"She's got a shotgun!" Shelly screamed.

Conrad swerved into the truck, but it was too late. The gunshot blew out the left front tire and sent the van reeling. Vicki and Shelly screamed as Conrad fought to keep control. He slammed on the brakes, and both vehicles shot past them. The van skidded into a ditch and toppled over.

Vicki unbuckled first and checked Conrad and Shelly. Shelly was bruised but okay. Conrad lay slumped over the steering wheel, his air bag deployed.

"Are you okay?" Vicki said.

Conrad grabbed his neck and put his head back. "I think so. But I can't say the same for the van. We're stuck."

"Look!" Shelly shouted.

The car and truck were turning. Shelly tried to open the side door, but it was stuck. Conrad pulled himself free and pushed the front passenger door open. The three crawled out and hit the ground just as the truck skidded to a stop in front of them.

Judd prayed as he watched Mr. Stein walk toward the Jerusalem Global Community headquarters. The man seemed fearless.

Sam stared at his father and stood. Lionel and Judd grabbed him and pulled him into his chair.

"We don't need anybody else getting arrested," Lionel said.

Mr. Stein walked into the street, his face turned toward the steps of the station. A car passed him and honked, but Mr. Stein continued, staring at the deputy commander and Sam's father. Mr. Stein stopped in the middle of the street and raised his voice. "You who walk in darkness, behold, you will see a great light—a light that will shine on all who live in the land where death casts its shadow."

Deputy Commander Woodruff and Mr. Goldberg turned and glared.

"This is what the Lord Almighty says," Mr. Stein continued. "'Every word that was written, every promise given, will be fulfilled.'"

Deputy Commander Woodruff walked down a few steps and yelled back, "And this is what I say; you are under the arrest of the Global Community!"

Judd looked at Lionel. "What's he doing?"

Lionel shrugged. "Looks like he wants them to take him away."

Mr. Stein stood his ground as GC officers walked outside to see what was going on. The deputy commander pointed and ordered them to arrest Mr. Stein.

"The captives will be released and the prisoners will be freed!" Mr. Stein shouted.

"And you will be behind bars where you belong, you stupid fool," Woodruff said. "No more of your lies after today."

The officers reached the bottom of the steps and moved into the street. Sam shook his head. "I don't understand."

Suddenly, officers coughed and gasped for air. One pulled a handkerchief from his back pocket and put it over his face. The two near Mr. Stein fell to their knees, sputtering and panting.

"What's that smell?" the deputy commander said. Everyone in front of the GC station coughed and waved their arms.

The waiter at the restaurant ran inside. "Sulfur! It's sulfur!" He closed the door behind him and collapsed in a heap.

A woman ran by them on the sidewalk shouting, "We're going to die! It's poison!"

"I don't smell anything," Sam said.

Then Judd saw them. The huge beasts rode

over a building in front of them. Judd
pointed. Lionel and Sam couldn't speak.

The horses approached the street where
Mr. Stein stood. They hovered as if walking
on air. These were not ordinary sized horses.
These were monsters. Judd had seen Clydes-
dales close up, but these were enormous, at
least twice the size of any he had ever seen.

Lionel gasped. "Look at their faces!"

Judd couldn't keep his eyes off them. Their
heads looked like lions with flowing manes
and huge teeth. Flames and thick yellow
smoke shot out of their mouths and nostrils,
but Judd didn't hear anything. No hoofbeats
or snorting or any sound.

The horses were so frightening, Judd almost
didn't notice the riders. They were every bit as
large as the animals. They looked human, but
each one was at least ten feet tall and five
hundred pounds. Every horseman wore a
shimmering breastplate. Their biceps and fore-
arms rippled with muscles as they worked to
control the enormous horses. Judd thought
they might stampede at any moment.

Judd jumped out of his chair. "Come on!"

"I'm not going out there," Sam said.

"These have to be the horses from Revelation 9. Tsion teaches that they won't hurt
believers."

"How can we be sure? They look pretty mean."

Judd raced into the street. Lionel and Sam followed. Mr. Stein put up a hand as the three came near. One of the horses was only a few yards away. It turned and for the first time they saw the tail.

"Sick!" Lionel said.

Instead of hair, a snake's head writhed on the end of the tail. It bared its fangs and looked at the kids.

"So this is why you came out here," Judd said to Mr. Stein. "You knew this was going to happen."

"I had no idea," Mr. Stein said. "I felt God wanted me to speak and I did. Follow me."

"We can walk right through the horses?" Judd said.

"These are not physical beings. Their effect is real. They will cause the deaths of many, but we have no reason to fear them."

Sirens wailed throughout the city as Judd and the others walked up the steps. The deputy commander lay on the steps, clutching his throat. As Judd passed, Woodruff reached out and grabbed his leg. Judd quickly jerked away. The man summoned his strength and stood, finally recognizing Judd. He reached for the radio on his shoulder and clicked the button.

Woodruff gasped and tried to speak.

Before he could utter a word, a horse moved toward them and turned, its tail crashing into Woodruff's back. The man flew into the air like a child's toy and crashed into the building. His limp body fell to the sidewalk.

Judd shuddered. How could the horses strike with such force when they weren't physical beings? He and the others had walked directly through them!

Lionel reached the deputy commander's body and checked his pulse. He shook his head.

"Let's go," Mr. Stein said.

🌵

Vicki started to run, but Conrad grabbed her arm.

"Stay right where you are!" the man in the truck said. Vicki noticed a gun rack in the rear of the pickup. The man stepped out and walked in front of the headlights. He was thin and had a long face with a stubbly beard. His arms were gangly, and he walked with a slight limp. He cocked a pistol and held it out as the car arrived.

"How many are there?" the woman said as she stepped out of the car. She was short and wore a leather jacket. She waved the shotgun as she talked.

"Three," Long Face said. "Two girls and a guy."

The driver of the car was a man in his mid-thirties. He was stocky with curly hair. He got out and eyed Vicki and Shelly. Something didn't seem right about him.

The woman threw a bag in front of Conrad. "Put all your Nicks and valuables in there and step away from the van."

"We don't have much," Vicki said. "This isn't even our car—"

"Shut up and do what you're told!" the woman screamed.

Conrad turned to Vicki and said, "Give them what they want. Main thing is getting out of here alive."

"Why didn't you think of that back on the road?" the woman yelled.

"Yeah," the man by the car whined. "You almost scratched my car."

Conrad shrugged. "The stuff's going to be hard to get. Van's all smashed and—"

The woman pointed the shotgun at Conrad. "Shut up and get out of the way."

Long Face crawled inside the van and rummaged around. He threw out Vicki's notebook, and papers flew everywhere. Vicki started to retrieve them, but Conrad held her back.

"I've got a bad feeling about this," Shelly whispered.

"Hey, look what I found!" Long Face said from the van. He handed a metal box to the woman.

"So, you were holding out on us!" the woman said. "Where's the key?"

Conrad pulled a key from his pocket and tossed it to her. She tried to catch it, but it pinged off the side of the car. The curly-headed man glared at him.

The box held enough Nicks to get the kids back to the schoolhouse, but not much more. The woman stuffed the money in her jacket pocket.

"Van's torn up," Long Face said. "Probably couldn't drive it even if we got it out of the ditch."

The woman kicked the van and cursed. "We could have sold it, no problem. Now it's a hunk of junk."

"Better make 'em pay for their mistake," the curly-headed man said. He stepped forward and reached for the shotgun.

The woman pushed him away and waved the gun at the kids. "If you hadn't tried to get away, we'd have let you go."

"We won't tell anybody what happened," Shelly said.

The woman frowned and pointed to the field. "Start walking."

"What are you going to do?" Conrad said.

"Move," Curly Hair said.

"You think we should make a run for it?" Vicki whispered.

"I don't think we have much choice," Conrad said.

Shelly gasped. "Wait. They're back!"

Vicki's mouth dropped open when she saw the horses and riders. A herd was moving effortlessly across the field behind them. Fire blew from the horses' nostrils, and great clouds of black and yellow smoke came from their mouths. Vicki guessed they were a half mile away.

The woman glanced behind her when Shelly gasped. The men did too. Both turned and laughed.

"You're not going to get us to fall for that," Long Face said.

"You don't see them?" Vicki said.

"Real cute," Curly said. "Just keep moving."

"If I were you, I'd get out of here fast," Conrad said.

"This is far enough," the woman said. "I'm tired of your games. Let's get this over with."

Vicki looked at the horses. They were right behind the three bandits, hovering over the field. Vicki cringed when she saw their faces. The locusts had been hideous, but these horses and their riders were even scarier.

"Whoa, what's that smell?" Long Face said.

Curly took a deep whiff of air and coughed violently. One of the horses blew a plume of smoke toward the three, and it engulfed them. The woman dropped the shotgun and fell to her knees. She grabbed her throat with both hands and gasped.

Long Face ran toward the kids, his face turning blue. He nearly knocked Shelly over as he pushed past them. One of the horses followed and snorted a blast of white-hot fire. Long Face burst into flames and went rolling headlong onto the ground.

Curly ran toward the road and jumped in the pickup truck. He gunned the engine and shot past several horses. One turned and flicked its snakelike tail and smashed the windshield. The truck went out of control, ran up the side of an embankment, and hit a tree. One snort from the horse's nostrils and the pickup was engulfed in flames.

The woman tried to stand but couldn't. Finally, she cried and stretched out on the ground. Her body twitched and jerked for a moment; then she lay still.

Shelly put her head on Vicki's shoulder

and cried. "I never dreamed it would be this awful."

Conrad checked, but the woman was dead. He found their money in her jacket and walked toward the road. "Come on, let's get out of here."

FOUR

Breaking News

MARK Eisman and the others at the schoolhouse sat in front of the small television their friend Z had recently sent. Mark usually monitored the computer for the latest news, but everyone wanted to see the local coverage. Darrion had alerted Mark about the horses and riders. Now they all sat before the flickering television.

"Reports from Rockford to downstate Illinois have officials concerned," a nervous reporter said. "But it's not just the Midwest that's being affected. We're hearing about fires and deadly fumes from around the globe. As of yet, there is no explanation for this lethal outbreak that has killed thousands. We have no word yet on the exact number of casualties, but some experts believe hundreds of thousands might lose their lives."

"Try millions," Darrion said.

Charlie sighed. "I'm sure glad I got the mark before any of this happened."

Someone handed the reporter a piece of paper. "We're going to join live coverage from the international headquarters of Global Community Network News."

The feed switched to a newscast already in progress. The anchor was better dressed than the local reporter but equally baffled at the unfolding events. "Emergency medical professionals are at a loss, frantic to determine the cause. Here's the head of the Global Community Emergency Management Association, Dr. Jurgen Haase."

Dr. Haase looked composed, almost too calm for the situation. He spoke slowly and with great poise. "If these deaths were isolated, we might say they were caused by a natural disaster, a rupture of some natural gas. But they seem random, and clearly the fumes are lethal. We urge citizens to use gas masks and work together to put out the fires."

The news anchor asked, "Which is more dangerous, the black smoke or the yellow?"

Haase said, "First we believed the black smoke was coming from the fires, but that doesn't appear to be the case. It can be deadly, but the yellow smoke smells of sulfur and has the power to kill instantly."

"Has the Global Community considered the possibility of terrorist action?"

"It's very early," Haase said. "We've ruled nothing out. We do know there is a group of religious zealots who would love to create more suffering, but I won't speculate on that. To be honest, we simply don't know what we're dealing with."

"Great," Darrion said. "Now we're being accused of germ warfare."

The reporter put a hand to his ear, then read from a bulletin. "This just in. While there are pockets in which no fire or smoke or sulfur has been reported, in other areas the death count is staggering, now estimated in the millions. His Excellency, Global Community Potentate Nicolae Carpathia, will address the world via radio and television and the Internet inside this half hour."

"What do you think Carpathia will say?" Lenore said.

Mark shook his head. "He'll find a way to look good. He'll probably get more people to worship him because of this."

The report switched to a feed from Jerusalem. Smoke rose from the old city, and fires were everywhere. Another report came from New Babylon, where Nicolae Carpathia was about to speak. People lay motionless in the street. Once sparkling buildings were shrouded in black and yellow clouds. Fire and smoke appeared on every continent, in every major city, but no one knew how it was happening. People throughout the world panicked. Airplanes filled with passengers plunged from the sky after choking pilots radioed their Maydays.

"They even have power to affect airplanes?" Charlie said.

Melinda walked in, rubbing her eyes. "What's going on?"

Lenore stood and let the girl have her seat. "The next judgment is here. Nicolae's about to put his spin on it."

"How do you know this is from God?" Melinda said.

Lenore showed her the passage in Revelation. Melinda read it and glanced at the television. "If this is supposed to be caused by horses, how come they haven't shown any?"

Mark said, "My guess is they're not visible. But believe me, they're real. And we don't know how long they'll be here. You could be in danger."

"Just me? Why wouldn't you guys be worried?"

Darrion turned down the volume. "When things like this happen, those who believe in Jesus are immune. The locusts didn't sting believers, just unbelievers. It's the same with this."

Melinda seemed in a daze. She stood and walked up the stairs to the balcony. Mark followed. The moon was bright, but there was no sign of horses and riders.

"You've heard the message every way we can think of telling you," Mark said. "We've all been praying for you."

"I want to talk to Vicki. I trust her, and I don't want to do something simply because I'm scared of dying."

"I understand. The problem is, we have no idea where she is. We haven't been able to reach her."

"I'll wait."

Darrion yelled that Carpathia was about to speak. Mark and Melinda sat just as the potentate was being announced. Carpathia looked into the camera and did his best to calm viewers.

"I want to assure you that this situation will soon be under control," Carpathia said. "We are working around the clock and using every resource to stop the fires and smoke. Meanwhile, I ask citizens of the Global Community to report suspicious activity, particularly anyone who is making or transporting toxic chemicals. Sadly, we have reason to believe that religious rebels may be behind this massacre of innocent lives. We have extended every courtesy to these people, and this is how they react."

Carpathia bit his lip. "Though they cross us at every turn, we have defended their right to dissent. Yet they continue to see the Global Community as an enemy. They feel they have a right to maintain an intolerant, close-minded cult that excludes anyone who disagrees with them.

"You have the right to live healthy, peaceful, and free. While I remain against war, I pledge to rid the world of this cult, beginning with the Jerusalem Twosome, who even now express no remorse about the widespread loss of life that has resulted from this attack."

"Who's he talking about?" Melinda said.

"Jerusalem Twosome must be his new nickname for the two prophets, Eli and Moishe," Mark said.

Carpathia pushed a button, and a video of Eli and Moishe appeared. They were speaking in unison near the Wailing Wall. Words flashed across the screen underneath the video clip.

"Woe to the enemies of the most high God!" they said. "Woe to the cowards who shake their fist at their creator and are now forced to flee his wrath! We beseech you, snakes and vipers, to see even this plague as more than judgment! Yea, it is yet another attempt to reach you by a loving God who has run out of patience. There is no more time to woo you. You must hearken to his call, see that it is he who loves you. Turn to the God of your fathers while there is still time. For the day will come when time shall be no more!"

Carpathia turned off the video and smiled. "The day will come, my friends, when these two shall no longer spread their venom. They shall no longer turn water to blood, hold back rain from the clouds, send plagues to the Holy Land and the rest of the globe. I upheld my end of the bargain negotiated with them months ago, allowing certain rebels to go unpunished. Now this is how we are repaid for our generosity.

"But the gift train stops here, loyal citizens. Your patience and steadfastness shall be repaid. The day will yet come when we will live as one world, one faith, one family of man."

"Yeah, one big happy family," Darrion said. "What a loser."

Carpathia continued. "We shall live in a utopia of peace and harmony with no more war, no more bloodshed, no more death. In the meantime, please accept my deepest personal condolences over the loss of your loved ones. They shall not have died in vain. Continue to trust in the ideals of the Global Community, in the tenets of peace, and in the genius of an all-inclusive universal faith that welcomes the devout of any religion.

"Just four months from now we shall celebrate in the very city where the preachers now taunt and warn us. We shall applaud their demise and revel in a future without plague and disease and suffering and death. Keep the faith, and look forward to that day. And until I address you again, thank you for your loyal support of the Global Community."

"What does that mean?" Melinda said.

"Tsion has taught us all along that the two witnesses will one day be killed by Carpathia. It looks like Nicolae has done his homework. The 1,260 days of their preaching ends in four months."

※

Mr. Stein led the kids inside the Global Community police station. Many of the officers had rushed outside when Mr. Stein began to speak. A few were still inside now, coughing and sputtering.

"Where's Sam?" Judd said.

"Outside with his dad," Lionel said. "I'll get him."

Mr. Stein pointed to a locked doorway. Judd found the keys on an officer's desk. Inside, they heard more coughing and wheezing.

"Can't breathe!" someone shouted. "We need air!"

Judd found Nada's cell. She was huddled in the corner with her mother. "Thank God you've come!" Nada said. She hugged Judd and pointed toward the back of the building where her father and brother were being kept.

As they rushed past the cells, several believers called out from behind the bars. Judd freed those with the mark of the believer on their foreheads. Most of them believed because Sam had given them the gospel.

Judd opened the last door on the corridor and found a guard on the floor, gasping for air. Kasim and Jamal cried when they saw Nada. She took the keys from Judd and released them. They had bruises on their faces, deep circles under their eyes, and they looked like they hadn't eaten for days.

"Let's get out of here," Jamal said weakly.

"Wait!" someone said as he rushed through the door.

Judd turned and spotted the jailer pointing his gun at them. "Stop or I'll shoot!"

Vicki crawled into the van and handed
Conrad and Shelly as many supplies as they
could pack into the sports car. The cell phone
had crashed into the windshield and was
fried. The sports car was a tight fit for the
three of them, but they were grateful to have
something to drive.

"I feel guilty taking this car," Vicki said.

"They're not going to use it anymore,"
Conrad said.

"I know, but they probably stole it."

Shelly pointed out the window at another
cavalry of fiery horses and riders. They were
moving north along an abandoned railroad
track. As they ran, they breathed great clouds
of black and yellow smoke over rows of
homes and ranches nearby. In some homes,
lights came on and people burst through the
front doors, falling on lawns and rolling. In
other places, the horses snorted enough fire
to send whole blocks up in smoke. Conrad
pointed to the other side of the road where
another herd stood perched on a butte over-
looking a small town.

"There doesn't seem to be any method,"
Shelly said. "They're just putting that smoke
and fire wherever they find people."

"I'm glad they came when they did,"

Conrad said. "I feel like a cat who's just used up two or three of its lives."

"How long will it be until we get home?" Vicki said.

"Before the roads were torn up during the earthquake, we'd have been able to do it in less than twenty hours," Conrad said. "Now it's going to be at least two days, and that's if we push it."

Vicki sat back and watched the herds run. She had no idea how long they would stay, but when they were through, the world would never be the same.

🌾

Judd held up his hands and begged the man not to shoot. The others stood back, waiting to see what would happen.

The guard choked and gasped for air. "If they find prisoners missing from here, they'll have me shot!"

Mr. Stein moved forward and knelt beside the man. "Many of your fellow officers are dead or are dying because of this judgment."

"You're one of those crazies!"

"I bring you good news. You don't have to die. Believe on the Lord Jesus and you will be saved."

The jailer frantically looked around. Some

of the prisoners were coughing uncontrollably. Others lay motionless in their bunks. "Why aren't *you* coughing? Is this some kind of spell you've put over the jail?"

Mr. Stein shook his head. "This was predicted thousands of years ago in the Scriptures. A third of those still living will die because of this terrible judgment. But you can be saved from it if you will—"

The jailer stood and waved the gun frantically. "All right, everybody back in their cells."

Mr. Stein moved back. He motioned for the others to leave the cellblock. "The Lord has provided a way of escape. I won't allow our friends, who are innocent, to suffer any longer."

The jailer coughed again and put his hand to his mouth. Mr. Stein turned to leave. The jailer raised the gun.

Before Judd could react, Nada lunged at the man. People screamed and fell to the floor as muffled gunfire echoed through the jail.

FIVE

Devastating News

For a few seconds, everything went into slow motion for Judd. Nada staggered backward and slumped to the floor. The jailer coughed and waved the gun around. Mr. Stein subdued the man and took the gun away.

Judd rushed to Nada's side and pulled her close. He pushed the hair from her face and saw a red spot appear on her shirt.

Jamal knelt beside his daughter and screamed, "No!"

Nada's mother burst into tears.

Judd felt Nada's neck. "She's alive. I can feel a pulse."

Nada coughed and struggled to breathe. Jamal leaned over her. "Daughter, speak to us."

Nada's eyelids fluttered. "Hard to . . . breathe . . ."

"Lie still," Jamal said.

"Somebody get a doctor!" Kasim shouted. "She's losing blood!"

Jamal and Kasim ran into the next room. Judd shook with fright. He didn't know what to do.

"Judd?" Nada whispered.

"I'm right here."

"I can't feel anything. My legs and arms won't work."

"You're going through a big shock. Just . . . we'll get some help."

Nada opened her eyes. "I had it all planned. We were going to spend . . . the rest of our lives . . ."

"Why did you do that?" Judd said.

Nada ignored his question. "Promise me you won't forget."

"Don't talk like that! You're going to be all right. We'll get a doctor and . . ."

Nada took another painful breath. "Go to your friends . . . take Sam and Lionel."

Nada's mother knelt and wept by the girl's side. She took Nada's limp hand and kissed it. A trickle of blood ran from the corner of Nada's mouth. Judd dabbed it with his shirt.

Nada looked at her mother and smiled. A tear ran down her cheek. She tried to speak but couldn't.

Nada let out a breath and rested her head on Judd's chest. He felt Nada's neck, then her wrist. Nothing. He held her body tightly and cried.

The air seemed to go out of the room. Judd's mind spun. He wanted to run, to hide, to get away from this awful scene. But here he was, holding the body of his friend. She had given her life for him and the others. How could he ever thank her? Or forgive her?

Jamal and Kasim rushed in with a stretcher. They stopped when they saw Judd's face. Nada's mother lay on the floor, weeping. Jamal and Kasim both collapsed beside Nada's body.

"I'm so sorry," Judd managed.

Mr. Stein, who had been standing nearby, knelt beside the group and placed a hand on Nada's head. "Father, we commend the spirit of our sister to you. We are thankful you allowed us the privilege of knowing her. She was filled with courage and truth. You have said that there is no greater love than for someone to lay down their life for a friend. Surely, Nada has done this today. Comfort us now with this loss, and we look forward to the day when we will be united again when you return to rule and reign."

Jamal picked up the prayer through his tears. "Oh, God, we were not worthy to have had her as a daughter. But we thank you for giving her to us. Now we give her back to you."

"If she hadn't found me, Lord," Kasim said, "I'd still be in New Babylon. Forgive me for rejecting your message through her for so long."

Nada's mother couldn't speak. She shook her head and wept at the girl's side. Judd squinted and tried to speak. Mr. Stein put a hand on his shoulder. Finally, Judd managed a few words. "God, she cared so much for her family. I thank you that I got to know her." Judd paused, then said, "If I'd only . . ."

Jamal put a hand on Judd when he couldn't continue. The man whispered, "It's okay, my brother. It wasn't your fault."

The jailer appeared behind Mr. Stein, walking like a drunk man. He approached the group staggering and coughing, clutching his throat. Mr. Stein turned and stood in time to catch him as the man collapsed.

Jamal and Kasim brought the stretcher, but it was too late. The jailer had been overcome by the smoke of the horses.

Jamal took Nada from Judd and carried her body outside. When Lionel saw them, his mouth dropped open. Judd told him briefly what had happened and asked about Sam.

"Over there." Lionel pointed.

Sam sat on the sidewalk, cradling his

father's head. The herd of horses had moved on, leaving the street littered with bodies. Lionel put an arm around Judd. "I'm really sorry about Nada."

Judd nodded.

"I've been trying to get Sam to move, but he won't budge."

"I'll talk with him."

Judd sat by Sam and put an arm around his shoulders.

"I prayed for him every day," Sam said. "I thought for sure he would believe . . ."

After a few moments, Judd said, "I don't have any more answers than you. I know God's in control, but I sure don't know how this all works together."

Mr. Stein said, "We should go."

"I can't leave my father like this!"

"The surviving GC will be back to lock down the jail," Kasim said.

Judd held up a hand. "We'll use the stretcher to carry his body."

Judd and Lionel carried Sam's father on the stretcher, and Jamal and Kasim carried Nada. They walked through streets littered with the dead. Some buildings were on fire, but there was no one to put them out. The massacre got worse as they neared Yitzhak's home. Those who hadn't been killed ran into the streets, wailing and crying over the dead.

Yitzhak contacted a funeral director about the bodies. "If you want a burial, you'll have to do it yourself," the man said. "The Global Community says they're going to burn the bodies to reduce the risk of contamination."

While Nada's mother prepared the bodies, Judd and Lionel found a pair of shovels in a utility building. The men took turns digging in the small backyard. Judd was numb. Each shovelful of dirt was a painful reminder that Nada no longer lived. When the holes were dug, everyone gathered outside.

"We have said our good-byes," Mr. Stein said softly. "But I need to add something. The time is coming when the Antichrist will take full control of the world system. The judgments will get worse. Before us are two people—one who knew God and one who didn't. One who showed the love of God, who gave her life so that we would be saved. May these two lives renew our resolve to live for God. We must let nothing stand in our way in telling others the truth. Even if it costs our lives."

"Amen," Sam said.

"Amen," the others said.

Sam grabbed a handful of dirt and tossed

it on his father's body. Each person did the same.

Before Judd went into the house, Nada's mother came to him and put something wrapped in cloth in his hand. "She would have wanted you to have this."

Judd couldn't speak.

Nada's mother said, "She told me some things about you two. I encouraged her to tell you what was in her heart, but she never had the chance. Some of it is in this letter. Take it."

Judd stuffed the package in his pocket and went upstairs. He sat on his bed and thought of all that had happened since the disappearances. Losing his family was tough. It had thrown him together with brothers and sisters of a different kind. Now that family was being torn apart. He closed his eyes and thought of each person, believer and unbeliever, who was no longer alive. The longer he lived, the more people he would lose.

When will it be my turn? Judd thought.

He let his mind wander until it finally came to rest on Nada. He had been so excited to free her. She was so close. Judd thought through the series of events. If he had only been quicker and lunged at the jailer before Nada, she might be alive. A wave of guilt swept over him. He hadn't pulled the trigger, but he felt responsible for Nada's death. Then came the anger. Maybe the man wouldn't have fired at all. If Nada had stayed where she was, perhaps no one would have been hurt.

Judd remembered the first time he had met Nada. He thought of their exercises and discussions on the roof of her father's building. They loved to talk late into the night. A lump rose in his throat. *Gone. Nada is really gone, and she isn't coming back.*

Judd pulled out the cloth-wrapped package. Inside was a folded piece of paper and Nada's necklace. On the gold chain was a cross. Judd turned it around and saw Nada's initials on the back. He held the cross to his lips, then slipped the necklace around his neck. The paper was worn and somewhat faded. Judd looked at the date at the top of the page and realized Nada had written the letter soon after her family's arrest.

> *Dear Judd,*
> *My mother suggested I write this down so I won't forget. Maybe the GC is going to execute us, and if that happens, you can take comfort in the fact that I'm in a better place. Being with Christ is what our lives are all about. If they've killed me, I'm there, so don't be sad for me. I love you very*

*much. From the moment you came to our
family, I felt close to you. You were like a
brother to me. Then, as my feelings grew
deeper, you were more than that.*

*But I have to tell you something. I feel
it's only fair that I express this. As close as
we became, in our talks and the time we
spent together, I always felt there was something missing. I couldn't put my finger on it
until we came back to Israel and you
backed away. I feel what I'm about to say is
something that God wants me to say. I have
prayed many nights about this. . . .*

Lionel knocked on the door and walked
in. "Care for some company?"

Judd folded the paper and put it in his
pocket. "Sure."

Lionel sat on the bed. "Sam's taking it
pretty hard about his dad. How about you?"

"I'm not exactly throwing a party."

"Yeah." Lionel put his hands on his knees.
"Well, I've got something to say. It might not
be the right time, but with the way things are
going, we don't know what's going to happen next."

"Say it."

"I rode you pretty hard about getting back
to the States. Said some bad stuff."

"You were right."

"Maybe. But I shouldn't have questioned your motives about Nada. I can't tell you how sorry I am about what happened."

"Thanks."

"However long it takes, whatever kind of time you want to spend with her family, even if you decide to stay, I'm with you."

Judd's lip quivered. He and Lionel had been together since the disappearances. Through the tough times with Lionel's uncle André, to the first printing of the *Underground*, and all that had gone on afterward, Lionel was there like a rock. Judd threw his arms around his friend and hugged him.

Judd told Lionel the full story about Nada and the jailer and how he was feeling.

"Man, you can't blame yourself."

"Who else?"

"It was instinct. She moved a little faster, that's all. Her family doesn't hold it against you. They're down there talking about you like you were their son."

"What kind of son would let his sister get killed?"

Lionel put a hand on Judd's shoulder. "We're going to get through this. You and Sam and Nada's family are going to come out on the other side."

"I don't know how."

"Time. Take as much as you need. Come get me if you want to talk."

When Lionel closed the door, Judd pulled out Nada's letter. What was it she was trying to tell him? Judd read:

> *I have prayed many nights about this. I've asked God to show me why I'm feeling this way. Honestly, I think something is holding you back. At first, I thought it was God. You're so sold out on him, and you want to live for him. But the more I thought and prayed, it became clear that God wasn't coming between us. I really believe there is someone else. You've never talked much about your friends in the States, but I sense there is someone there you care about deeply.*
>
> *Maybe I'm making this up. If so, I apologize. But if I'm right and you find this letter, go back to her. You're a wonderful person with so much to offer. I have loved being your friend. I'm sorry for the trouble I caused you in New Babylon. I'm sorry for being difficult at times. (You had your moments too.) I'll look forward to seeing you again, whether it's in this life or the next. May God bless you.*
>
> *Love,*
> *Nada*

Judd folded the letter and shook his head. A thousand thoughts swirled in his head. *Is she right? Did I hold back in our relationship? Why?*

Judd lay back on the bed. The shock of seeing the horses and the experience at the jail had drained him of emotion and strength. He didn't think he could sleep, but when he closed his eyes, he drifted off and dreamed of Nada.

SIX

Death Toll

VICKI listened closely to the reports about the deadly horses as they drove east. Through Nebraska they saw the effects of the latest judgment. Houses in Lincoln were charred. The kids drove through billowing yellow and black smoke that floated through the area. They spotted herds of horses and riders in Omaha.

"I hope I never see those horses again," Shelly said.

Conrad turned the news down. "I don't get it. Those beasts are evil. They must want to hurt believers."

"God's using those killing machines for his own purpose. Somehow he's put a hedge around those who are his, and those beings know it."

Though it was a lot smaller than the van, the kids slept in the car as much as they could. In Iowa City, they rented two motel rooms with most of their remaining money. Conrad staggered to his room. "I'm going to sleep, and I'm not waking up for a week."

Vicki and Shelly tried to order a pizza, but they couldn't get an answer at any restaurants. Instead, they walked half a block to a convenience store and bought snacks.

"This used to be my favorite thing to do on vacation," Shelly said. "My mom would give me a few dollars and send me to a store next to the hotel. I'd get all kinds of soda and junk food, then stay up all night watching television."

Vicki smiled. "We used to have fun at the vending machines. I'd take my little sister, and we'd get pop and candy. Sometimes the machines would give us more than we'd paid for, and we felt like kings."

Shelly flicked on the television as Vicki spread their food on one of the beds. Many of the channels carried updates on the incredible world situation.

"Scientists are still speculating on the cause of this worldwide death plague," one news anchor said. "Hundreds of thousands are reported dead; millions have been sickened by the mysterious smoke that seemingly came out of nowhere."

"They can't see the horses," Shelly said.

Vicki shook her head. "Somehow God made them visible to us but blinded unbelievers."

Reports from overseas showed horrific scenes in major cities on every continent. People lay dead in the streets. One amateur video showed a man standing on a street corner in Brussels. Smoke rose in the distance, and people ran in fear. One second the man stood by a lamppost. The next instant he was flying through the air, smashing into a huge window. They showed the video again in slow motion, but there were no clues as to how the man had moved so quickly.

One expert guessed that the earth was going through "a strange gravitational change, which makes some areas at risk for life-threatening events."

"They don't have a clue," Vicki said.

Shelly tried other channels. Those that weren't showing the news were disgusting. One program featured a man in a desperate search for a family member who had been buried alive. A ticking clock was positioned at the bottom of the screen. At first, Vicki thought it was a movie.

"This is real," Shelly said in disbelief.

"Turn to something else."

Shelly switched to the next channel. A man in black robes and a mask stood inside a five-pointed star. It looked like he was praying.

"Turn it off," Vicki said.

Shelly did. "What was that?"

"Exactly what Tsion Ben-Judah predicted. People love themselves and their sin too much. Tsion said we'd see more drug use, murder, gross sexual stuff, and . . ."

"And what?"

"I think that guy was leading people in a prayer, but it wasn't to God. I think he was praying to demons."

Shelly shivered.

"The other channels are probably worse."

The girls lay in the dark, talking and trying to fall asleep, but the images they had seen on television were too much.

When the sun came up, Vicki and Shelly dressed and put their things in the car. They waited until they thought they heard Conrad moving around and knocked.

The kids ate some snacks and got back on the road. Vicki sat in front and let Shelly have the backseat so she could rest.

"You guys didn't sleep?" Conrad said.

Vicki shook her head. "How much longer until we're at the schoolhouse?"

"If we push hard enough, we could be there tonight."

🔆

Judd awoke to a quiet house. Yitzhak had asked everyone who was staying there to keep as quiet as possible out of respect for Nada's family and Sam. Judd found Nada's mother at the kitchen table alone. She pulled out a chair and said, "Sit."

The woman had said very little in Judd's presence since he had met her. He wondered if it was cultural or if she was ashamed of her English. Judd said, "All this time I've never known your first name."

The woman smiled. "Lina."

Judd nodded. "I read Nada's note. Did she write it in jail?"

"Yes. She told me a little about her concerns and said she wanted to talk to you when we were released. I told her she should write down her feelings so she would remember everything. I never dreamed she would die." Lina looked away and closed her eyes.

"I don't know if she was right," Judd said. "Maybe I was concerned about what your husband thought about us—"

"What about her belief that there is someone else?"

Judd sighed. "I have friends back home that
I met after the Rapture. But I'm not sure—"

Lina put a hand on Judd's shoulder.
"Forgive me. I do not like to give personal
advice when it's not asked for."

"Go ahead."

"Nada spoke very highly of you. She said
you were a gentleman in every way. But
she had a gift for knowing things. The
longer you two knew each other, the more
she felt like there was someone standing
between you and her. If this is true,
you must return to your home and find
out."

Judd ran a hand through his hair. The only
person he was remotely interested in was
Vicki, and they had fought so much. He didn't
know what to think.

"Jamal and I agree that you should stay
here as long as you need to. Frankly, it may
take a while to get back to the States with the
judgment that has come."

"Does your husband know about this?"

Lina shook her head. "All he knows is that
he has lost his only daughter. She was such
a joy to him. When she was a little girl, he
would take her everywhere. When he was at
work, she would wait at the window until

afternoon watching for him. It was very difficult for him when she became interested in you."

"That's why I tried to be careful. The trip to New Babylon was totally Nada's idea."

Lina smiled. "I understand. Even when she was small, she had wild ideas. She collected kangaroos. Stuffed. Porcelain. She cut out pictures of kangaroos and taped them to the wall of her bedroom. It was no surprise to me that she disappeared one day. We found her walking on the street, several blocks from our house, with a suitcase full of clothes and her kangaroos."

"Where was she going?"

"Australia. She had read an article in the newspaper that said there are many kangaroos there. She said she was prepared to take a bus if she got too tired."

Judd laughed out loud. That was Nada all right. Stowing away in a Global Community airplane was a piece of cake compared to her trip to Australia. "How old was she?"

"Seven, I think," Lina said, the tears starting again. "I believe you when you say it was her idea."

"I'm not sure how soon we'll go home. So if it's okay with your family then, I'd like to stay here awhile longer until we've arranged the flight."

Lina hugged Judd. "May God bless you and keep you safe."

※

Mark Eisman was excited to read anything Tsion Ben-Judah had posted on his Web site, but when Tsion sent him a personal note late one night, Mark was thrilled. The file attached was Tsion's latest message to fellow believers around the world.

I am sending you this a few hours before this hits the Web site, Tsion wrote. *Please work your magic to make it understandable to young people.*

Mark went to work and was almost finished when he heard Darrion sound an alarm. "There are headlights coming up the road!"

"Maybe it's Vicki and the others," Mark said, rushing to the balcony for a better look. Lenore wasn't far behind. Tolan cried downstairs.

"It's not them," Charlie shouted from the kitchen. "It looks like a small car. Could be GC!"

"Everybody to the basement," Mark yelled. "We take no chances."

As the others ran downstairs, Mark

unplugged the laptop and grabbed the important files.

"What's all the commotion?" Janie said, rubbing her eyes.

"Unknown car's coming up the road. Get to the hideout."

"Not me. I'm not going to that dungeon again."

"Fine. If it's the GC, you'll be the first one they catch."

Janie scrambled down the steps behind Mark. They were almost to the basement when Mark heard the car's horn. "The signal! It's Vicki!"

The kids rushed upstairs and greeted their friends. Vicki took Tolan in her arms and squeezed him tightly. "You're getting so big!"

Janie headed back to her room while everyone else settled in the kitchen.

"Don't you want to hear what happened?" Vicki said.

"Tell me in the morning," Janie said.

※

Vicki found Melinda and gave her a hug as she squeezed in with the others. She couldn't believe she was finally back among her friends.

Conrad explained what had happened to

the cell phone and the computer. Shelly
described what had happened with the
bandits in Colorado and how their van had
been totaled.

The newest believer, a girl named Jenni,
laughed and said, "I'll take the car over the
van any day."

"Did they take your money?" Lenore said.

Vicki described the interaction with the
three thieves. The kids gasped when they
heard the story of the horses and riders and
what they had done to the thieves.

Vicki took over and went through many of
the stops they had made across the country.
She wanted to tell the others about Jeff
Williams, but she knew she couldn't. "We
met a relative of someone in the Trib Force,"
Vicki said. "We need to pray for this guy and
his dad."

"Who is it?" Darrion said.

"I promised I wouldn't say."

Mark excused himself and returned a few
minutes later with a stack of pages an inch
thick.

"What's that?" Vicki said.

"Read it," Mark said. "It's feedback."

Vicki read the first page but couldn't
continue. She passed the stack to Shelly.

"These are messages from people we met?"
Shelly said.

"All but the last few pages," Mark said. "Those are more requests for you to come teach."

Vicki took the stack back and glanced through the pages. She recognized most of the names. Each person had a story to tell about how God had used Vicki, Conrad, and Shelly in their lives. "I don't know what to say," Vicki finally said.

"You can read those tomorrow," Mark said, pulling out another printout. "This is even more exciting."

"What is it?" Melinda said.

"Tsion Ben-Judah's latest message to believers." Mark looked at his watch. "It's supposed to be released on the Web in a few minutes. But I have an advance copy. And you're not going to believe what's in here."

SEVEN

Tsion's Message

VICKI wanted to sleep, but she wanted to hear what Tsion had said even more. As Mark read the letter, changed slightly for younger readers, she felt like she was taking a drink of cold water after a long journey across the desert.

"My dear brothers and sisters in Christ, my heart is heavy as I write to you. While the 144,000 evangelists raised up by God are seeing millions come to Christ, the one-world religion continues to become more powerful and—I must say it—more revolting. Preach it from the mountaintops and into the valleys: There is one God and one Mediator between God and man, the Man Christ Jesus.

"The deadly demon locusts prophesied in Revelation 9 finally died out after torturing millions. Many who were bitten at the end *of that plague have recovered only three months ago.*

"While many gave their lives to God after seeing this horrible judgment, most have become even more set in their ways. It should have been obvious to the leader of the Enigma Babylon One World Faith that followers of that religion suffered everywhere in the world. But we followers of Christ, the so-called rebels—enemies of tolerance—were spared."

Darrion shook her head. "Makes you wonder why anyone wouldn't believe the truth about God."

Vicki glanced at Melinda. The girl looked down at the table as Mark continued.

"We can be thankful that in this time of turmoil, our beloved preachers in Jerusalem continue to prophesy and win converts to Christ. They do this in that formerly holy city that now must be compared to Egypt and Sodom.

"By now you know that the sixth Trumpet Judgment, or the second woe of Revelation 9, has begun. I was correct in assuming the 200 million horsemen are spiritual and not physical beings. But I was wrong to think they would be invisible. I

have spoken with people who have seen these beings kill by fire and smoke and sulfur as the Scripture predicts. Yet unbelievers charge we are making this up."

"I saw them, and I never want to see them again," Shelly said.

"It is helpful to know this current plague was created by the releasing of four angels bound in the Euphrates River. We know that these are fallen angels, because nowhere in Scripture do we ever see good angels bound. These were apparently bound because they wanted to create chaos on earth. Now they are free to do so. In fact, the Bible reveals they were prepared for a specific hour, day, month, and year."

Melinda raised a hand. "I don't get it. I thought angels were good."

"They were all created by God to follow him," Vicki said. "But a third of the angels followed Satan and became demons. Angels only got one chance to choose."

"I'm glad I'm not an angel," Charlie said. "It took me a long time to decide to follow God."

"What's the deal with the river Tsion mentioned?" Shelly said.

"I'm getting to that," Mark said. He turned a page and read:

"It is significant that the four angels have been in the Euphrates. It is the most prominent river in the Bible. It bordered the Garden of Eden, was a boundary for Israel, Egypt, and Persia, and is often used in Scripture as a symbol of Israel's enemies. It was near this river that man first sinned, the first murder was committed, the first war fought, the first tower built in defiance against God, and where Babylon was built. Babylon is where idol worship started. The children of Israel were taken there as prisoners, and it is there that the final sin of man will culminate."

"That means Nicolae is going to get clobbered one day," Charlie said to Melinda. Mark smiled and continued.

"Revelation 18 predicts that Babylon will be the center of business, religion, and world rule, but also that it will eventually fall to ruin, for strong is the Lord God who judges her."

Mark moved to a blackboard and wrote:

R
25%
75%

25%
50%

"What do those numbers mean?" Shelly said.

"I studied what Tsion wrote and came up with this chart," Mark said.

"I'll bet the *R* is for Rapture," Darrion said.

"Right. Tsion told us the horses and riders will kill a third of the population alive right now." He pointed to the *R*. "After the Rapture came a great war, an earthquake, and meteors. All of that killed 25 percent of the people alive after the disappearances. That left 75 percent of the people who weren't taken away by God. Follow closely. One-third of 75 percent is 25 percent, so the current wave of death will leave only 50 percent of the people left behind at the Rapture."

Vicki shook her head. "And the worst is yet to come."

"This next section is a little difficult," Mark continued. "Tsion thinks God wants people to come to him, but this latest judgment might be preparation for the final battle between good and evil. He's weeding out the people who won't accept him."

"I don't understand," Shelly said.

"Let me read," Mark said.

*"The Scriptures foretell that those unbe-
lievers who do survive will refuse to turn
from their wickedness. They will insist on
continuing worshiping idols and demons,
and engaging in murder, sorcery, sexual
immorality, and theft. Even the Global
Community's own news operations report
that murder and theft are on the rise, and
idol and demon worship are actually
applauded in the new tolerant society."*

"So God is taking away people who would
be against him in the big battle?" Charlie said.

"Exactly," Mark said.

"So how much longer will the horsemen
be around?" Darrion said.

"Tsion believes it may continue four more
months, until the three-and-a-half-year anni-
versary of the treaty between Nicolae and
Israel."

"Which will also be the end of our friends
Eli and Moishe," Vicki said.

"They're going away?" Charlie said.

"In the due time, the Antichrist will
execute them," Vicki said. "But they won't
stay dead."

"Here's the bad news for us," Mark said,
finding his place in the letter.

"This will usher in a period when many more believers will be martyred."

"What's that mean?" Charlie said.

"Killed because you believe in Jesus," Conrad said.

The room fell silent. Vicki thought of the adult Tribulation Force and those believers who even work inside the Global Community. Could they survive for long when they were employed by the enemy of God? What about Buck Williams and Rayford Steele? Vicki closed her eyes and wondered how many in this room would make it to the Glorious Appearing of Christ.

"Let me finish the rest of this, and we'll get some sleep," Mark said.

"Many of you have written and asked how a God of love and mercy could pour out such awful judgments upon the earth. God is more than a God of love and mercy. The Scriptures say God is love, yes. But they also say he is holy, holy, holy. He is just, as in justice. His love was expressed in the gift of his Son as the means of salvation. But if we reject this love gift, we fall under God's judgment.

"I know that many hundreds of thousands of readers of my daily messages must

visit this site not as believers but as search-
ers for truth. So permit me to write directly
to you if you do not call yourself my brother
or sister in Christ. I plead with you as never
before to receive Jesus Christ as God's gift of
salvation. The sins that the stubborn unbe-
lievers will not give up will run out of con-
trol during the last half of the Tribulation,
referred to in the Bible as the Great Tribu-
lation.

"Imagine this world with half its popula-
tion gone. If you think it is bad now with
millions having disappeared in the Rapture,
children gone, services and conveniences
affected, try to fathom life with half of all
civil servants gone. Firemen, policemen,
laborers, executives, teachers, doctors,
nurses, scientists . . . the list goes on. We
are coming to a period where survival will
be a full-time occupation."

Vicki glanced at Melinda. She was hanging
on every word of Tsion's letter.

"I would not want to be here without
knowing God was with me, that I was on
the side of good rather than evil, and that
in the end, we win. Pray right now. Tell
God you recognize your sin and need
forgiveness and a Savior. Receive Christ

*today, and join the great family of God.
Sincerely, Tsion Ben-Judah."*

Mark folded the pages and put them in his pocket.

Lenore said, "You did a great job making that understandable." All the kids agreed, then, one by one, stood and headed off to bed.

Shelly hugged Conrad. "Thanks for all the driving you did."

"My pleasure, little lady," Conrad said in a mock cowboy voice. He laughed, and Shelly winked at Vicki.

"Wait a minute," Vicki whispered. "Are you interested in Conrad?"

Shelly yawned. "I'd love to stay up and talk, but I'm pretty tired."

"Not fair!" Vicki said, but Shelly was already out of the room.

Melinda sat alone at the table. Vicki put an arm around her. "You want to talk?"

"I don't trust the others like I do you."

"I'm glad you trust me."

"When they told me about those horses and riders, I freaked. Getting stung by the locust was bad enough, but this next thing sounds awful."

"It will be. It is. But you don't have to be afraid. If you'll just—"

"I know. All I have to do is believe like you guys." Melinda turned. "I don't want to do this simply because I'm scared."

"Understood, but God's trying to get your attention."

"He's doing a pretty good job of it." Melinda looked out the window. "I had nightmares after they told me."

"Nightmares?" Vicki said, stifling a smile. "What?"

Vicki put a hand to her head. "I'm sorry. I'm just really tired. We were talking about the horses, and you said you had night*mares*. Bad joke."

Melinda smiled. "You're crazy. That's one thing I like about you. A lot of church people I met would never laugh."

Vicki snorted and put a hand over her mouth. "My mom used to call this the tired sillies. We'd laugh our heads off late at night at the dumbest things."

When Vicki settled, Melinda said, "Maybe that's one thing that scares me. If I believe like you guys, I'm afraid I'll never have any fun again."

"I used to think the same thing. Church people seemed so stiff and uptight, like if they cracked a smile their face would break. But the believers I've met since the disappearances are the real deal. They're serious about their beliefs, but there's something different."

"They're happy on the inside."

Vicki nodded. "Yeah. God can give you joy, even in the middle of the worst things anyone on earth has faced. He puts something indescribable in your heart. He gives you hope."

Melinda nodded and looked away. "I want that," she whispered. "I don't want to live scared anymore. In my dreams, those horses had big hooves, and they were tromping all over people. One stood by my bed and breathed on me."

"To be honest, those horses and riders were even worse than your nightmares." Vicki described the heads of the horses, the tails, and the fire and smoke that came from their mouths and noses.

The more Vicki said, the more worried Melinda looked. "How can you see that and not be terrified?"

"I was. And so were Conrad and Shelly. But after we figured out it was a judgment from God, we knew we wouldn't get hurt."

Melinda brushed hair from her face. "You've done a lot for me. You helped me when Felicia died, when my feet got frostbitten, and even after those locusts bit me. I know you care."

"Believe me, God cares so much more for you than I ever could."

"Maybe I'm one of those weeds God's getting rid of," Melinda said.

"What do you mean?"

"In that letter from Dr. Ben-Judah, Mark said there were some people who would reject God and just go on doing what they wanted. Maybe I'm one of them."

Vicki put a hand on Melinda's shoulder. "I've seen how you listen when I teach. I saw you listening to the letter. I think you want to know God."

"I could never be as good as you and the rest."

"You don't have to be good—"

"If somebody came and tried to arrest me and threatened to kill me like I did to you guys, I'd never let them stay here. I'd have sent me back to the GC as fast as I could."

"Let God work on your heart, Melinda. You'll be surprised at what he can do. I was just like you. I thought religion was for people who had it all together. But God takes you like you are. He wants to come in and help change you from the inside out. He can take away the fear."

Melinda closed her eyes and clenched her teeth.

Vicki knew there was a battle raging. She felt Melinda needed a challenge. "What do you believe about Jesus?"

Melinda sighed. "I think . . . I think he was God, like you've said."

"Do you believe he died in your place, to take away your sin?"

"Not if I'm one of those weeds."

"Stop it," Vicki said. "Don't pass up this chance. I can tell God is working on you. Let him do it."

"Okay," Melinda said. She rolled up her sleeves and put her hands on her knees.

"Do you believe Jesus died for you?"

"Yeah, I think he did."

"He's offering you a gift right now. Do you want to accept it?"

Melinda paused, then looked up. "I'd like that a lot."

"Then pray with me."

As Vicki prayed, Melinda repeated the words. "God in heaven, I'm sorry for the bad things I've done. I believe you died in my place to pay for my sin. Right now I want to receive the gift of eternal life that you offer. Make me a new person. Be my Lord and my

Savior from this moment on. In Jesus' name.
Amen."

Melinda looked at Vicki and gasped.
"When did you get that thing on your forehead?"

EIGHT

Confrontation

JUDD kept to himself and tried to deal with Nada's death alone. He awoke in the middle of the night, sweating. The whole experience felt like a bad dream. Surely Nada would walk through the door any minute, and everything would be all right. But what had happened wasn't a dream. Each time he awoke and realized she was gone, he felt a stab in the heart.

Mr. Stein asked to speak with Judd. "When my wife died, it was very difficult. Since my daughter had left my faith and had become a believer in Christ, I felt alone. I responded to my wife's death by withdrawing. That wasn't all bad, but there came a point when I had to talk with someone."

Judd nodded. "I guess Sam is going through the same thing."

"Yes. He came to me yesterday, and we had a long talk. It is difficult for him since his father never responded to the message of Christ."

"That's a tough one. I know it'll be good to talk with someone, but I just don't feel . . ." Judd's voice trailed off.

"I am available when you're ready."

Lionel came in the room. "Did you hear what happened to Mac McCullum?"

"Mac who?" Mr. Stein said.

"The pilot who flew us to New Babylon," Judd said. "What's up?"

"A few days ago Mac's plane was attacked," Lionel said.

Judd raced to the computer and looked at the information Lionel had downloaded. The first reports were sketchy. Officials feared that the supreme commander, Leon Fortunato, and the others on the Condor 216 had all been killed by the mysterious smoke and fire. Later reports told a different story. The plane had landed in Johannesburg, South Africa, for a planned meeting with one of Nicolae Carpathia's regional potentates. It was ambushed by gunmen who believed Carpathia was on the plane. Mac McCullum was hailed a hero by Leon Fortunato.

Judd pulled up a video clip from a news conference Fortunato had held not long after the incident. "I was prepared for a meeting with Regional Potentate Rehoboth, but what

I received was nothing short of an assassination attempt. Though there was a hail of
bullets, I was able to escape. If it had not
been for the quick thinking of myself and the
flight crew, we would all be dead right now."

Fortunato praised Mac McCullum for
"putting his body between the would-be
assassins and myself." Fortunato promised a
ceremony honoring the pilots as heroes as
soon as they had recuperated from their
wounds.

"Why would Mac save Fortunato's life?"
Lionel said.

"I can't wait to talk to him and get the
inside scoop," Judd said.

Vicki slept until late the next afternoon. She
wanted to tell the others about Melinda. She
went to the kitchen to get something to eat
but found no one. The front room was
empty as well. Finally, Vicki discovered a
group of kids in the computer room. Mark
was leading them in a review of all of Tsion
Ben-Judah's Internet messages. Melinda was
in the middle of the group, listening intently.

Mark welcomed Vicki, and Melinda
beamed. "I asked to hear some of those
messages again," Melinda said. "I think a lot

of it went over my head the first time, but now it's making more sense."

Janie walked by and spotted Vicki. She yawned and said, "So, you're back. Great."

Melinda stepped forward. "I did it, Janie. I finally became a believer. You should too."

Janie shook her head. "Just what I need. Another Holy Roller who wants to sign me up." Janie looked at Vicki. "You guys don't quit, do you?"

Vicki bit her lip and kept quiet.

"You know the mark they've talked about?" Melinda said. "It's real. As soon as I finished praying, I saw it on Vicki's forehead."

"Sure you did," Janie said. She looked at the others and cursed. "Don't you think it's bad enough that we get stung by the worst-looking creatures ever to fly over the earth? Now you scare this girl into joining your little religious club."

"I don't believe this," Vicki muttered.

"It didn't happen that way," Melinda said. "I asked God to forgive me, and he did. He loves you, and he wants—"

Janie held up a hand. "Give it a rest. Haven't you seen all the people dying around the world? You think a loving God would allow that?"

"He's trying to get your attention," Melinda said.

"No. He's not there or he'd do something about all this. The only person you can trust right now is Nicolae Carpathia."

Melinda stood, a frightened look on her face. She went to the window.

"What is it?" Mark said.

"Something outside . . . I was right. There they are."

A herd of horses stood on the other side of the river. The riders looked toward the schoolhouse. Suddenly, a few of the horses moved over the water.

"They're coming!" Melinda gasped.

Janie looked out the window. "Who's coming? I don't see anything."

"We have to get her downstairs!" Melinda said. "It's her only hope."

Vicki reached for Janie, but the girl jerked away. "You're not taking me down there!"

Melinda grabbed Janie's arms and held them behind her. Janie struggled to get free, but Mark and Conrad grabbed her legs. Together they rushed the screaming girl down the stairs and into the lowest chamber of the schoolhouse.

Vicki watched in horror as the horses and riders moved effortlessly across the surface of the river. It was like seeing a horror movie. The riders didn't speak. They simply stared at the schoolhouse. The horses snorted smoke, but no fire. Vicki heard coughing and screaming below and rushed downstairs.

"She's having a hard time breathing!" Mark yelled. "Bring some wet cloths."

Vicki ran to the kitchen and found some towels and ran them under the water faucet. She jumped back as a horse stuck its lionlike head in the window. It gnashed its teeth and snarled.

Vicki took the cloths below. Janie grabbed them from her and put them over her mouth. The smoke had penetrated the walls of the house. The kids could see it, but they couldn't smell it.

Janie's tongue stuck out of her mouth as she coughed. It was clear the girl wouldn't last long if the smoke continued.

"We have to do something," Vicki said. She rushed upstairs and onto the balcony.

Lenore stood holding Tolan close to her chest. "They're huge," she whispered, "just like you said."

A ring of horses had circled the house. The rider in front of Vicki was right at eye level. She stared into the horseman's face. The being seemed angry and determined. He wore a brightly colored breastplate that gleamed in the sun. This small detachment of the demon army was there to destroy another unbeliever.

Vicki mustered her courage and spoke. "Leave this place now! In the name of Jesus Christ, the almighty God, I command you to leave."

The horseman's face was dark, like a bottomless pit. He turned and looked at Vicki, and she saw the monstrous, evil face with sharp teeth and a look that defied description.

Vicki turned away and closed her eyes. *Father, I ask you to send these things away. If they stay, there's no way Janie will ever become a believer. Please, have mercy on her and make these things leave.*

Suddenly, the horse reared and waved its hooves in the air. Fire shot from its nostrils and soared over the roof of the schoolhouse. The fire fell like molten lava on the ground, burning trees and bushes. The schoolhouse was unharmed.

The horseman controlled the demon animal and glared at Vicki. He didn't say anything, but he seemed to communicate with the others that it was time to leave. They turned from the house and followed the river until they were out of sight.

Janie had inhaled some of the foul-smelling smoke, but she was still alive when Vicki reached her. They brought her upstairs and tried to help her breathe. When she stopped coughing and gagging, she asked, "What happened?"

Melinda began to answer, but Vicki held up a hand. "Just rest and we'll talk about it later."

Downstairs, Melinda looked confused. "Don't you want her to believe?"

"I do," Vicki said, "but her heart is hard. I don't know what else God could do to soften it, but I know if we go in there and try to tell her some cosmic horsemen made her cough, she's going to laugh and say we're making it up."

"It took me a while to realize the truth," Melinda said. "Maybe she just needs a little more time."

"Which is what we don't have," Mark said. He called everyone together in the computer room. "I just got a message from Carl in Florida. He says the GC is going ahead with their plans for the satellite schools. A special order was sent out yesterday to the directors of the project to have their centers ready for students within the week."

"All this death and devastation and they're starting a school?" Lenore said.

"Carl said they want to put their own spin on what's going on."

Shelly shook her head. "A third of their classes are going to be gone before the horsemen get done."

"We need to figure out a plan about the school nearest us," Conrad said.

Mark scratched his chin. "Yeah, but there's something else Carl said that worries me."

Vicki looked over Mark's shoulder as he read the e-mail out loud. *"I told you that part of the reason the GC is starting these schools is to identify possible recruits for their Morale Monitors. Now they have something new brewing. I haven't been able to find out exactly what it is, but I'm positive it won't be good for believers."*

Vicki wondered what new things the GC could dream up to hurt believers. If Tsion Ben-Judah was right, the next few years were going to be anything but easy for those who followed Christ.

※

Judd slowly came out of his shell over the next few days. He went to Sam and sat with him for a few hours, not saying a word.

Finally, the boy opened up and talked about his father. "It feels like my prayers were wasted," Sam said. "I prayed so hard for him. What went wrong?"

"God wants people to know him, but he gives us a choice. You and I chose to accept God's gift. Your dad rejected it."

"I picture my father suffering now. I wish I could take his place."

Judd knelt by Sam. "This is going to hurt for a long time, but you're not responsible for your dad's choice. The only person God holds you responsible for is you. You can pray and plead with others, but it's their decision."

Sam nodded and thanked Judd. "You're right about it taking a long time. I can't imagine not feeling this ache in my heart."

"Yeah, me too."

Judd watched the news reports about the horsemen. Lionel, Sam, and the others gathered around when the ceremony was held in honor of Captain Montgomery (Mac) McCullum and Mr. Abdullah Smith. Leon Fortunato took the stage in front of thousands and explained that the attempt on his life was actually a planned assassination of Nicolae Carpathia.

"However, while the gunmen succeeded in destroying the plane and killing four staff personnel, heroic measures by both the pilot and first officer saved my life. The assassins died as a result of the immediate response by Global Community Peacekeeping Forces."

Judd noticed a slight smile on Mac's face as Leon talked.

"Is Abdullah a believer as well?" Mr. Stein asked.

"I think Mac mentioned that he was," Judd said.

Fortunato introduced Nicolae Carpathia. "We honor these brave men today. In the face of overwhelming odds and much fire-power, these two put their lives on the line for the good of the Global Community. On behalf of the loyal citizens of the Global Community, I thank you."

The crowd went wild as Mac and Abdullah stepped forward and shook hands with the potentate. "I present you now with the Golden Circle, the prize for valor, with thanks." Carpathia stood back, beaming.

As they watched the coverage, Judd scanned through other news he had missed. He sat up straight when he came upon infor-mation about a plane crash. It had been reported some time ago, but it still made him nearly sick to his stomach as he read it aloud.

"'A large private aircraft has crashed off the coast of Portugal. The plane's lone passenger was Hattie Durham, former personal assistant to Global Community Potentate Nicolae Carpathia. The pilot, Samuel Hanson of Baton Rouge, Louisiana, United States of North America, is also presumed dead.'"

"That's the Hattie we know, right?" Lionel said.

Judd nodded. "I have to talk to Mac about this."

NINE

Mac's Story

Judd dialed Mac's secure phone later that night.

Mac answered and said, "Is that you, Rayford?"

"It's Judd Thompson, Mr. McCullum."

"Hey, what a surprise! You guys finally make it to Israel?"

Mac grew silent as Judd explained what had happened to Nada and her family. Judd choked up twice as he recounted the events, but he finally got through it. Telling it to Mac was difficult, but it felt good for someone on the adult Trib Force to know what was going on.

"Well, I'm sure sorry to hear about Nada. She was a good kid. I admired her courage. We need more people like her. I'll ask Rayford and the others to pray for you and her family."

"I'd appreciate that, sir."

"It must be doubly tough after what happened to that Rudja guy."

"Pavel's dad?" Judd said. "What happened?"

"I'm sorry. I thought you knew. Something must have gone haywire at the funeral for his son. The GC kept it quiet, but they were hunting him for a couple of days afterward. They finally got a tip from one of his friends. Seems the guy was trying to tell him the truth about God and his friend ratted him out."

"Where is Mr. Rudja now?"

"They arrested him and charged him with rebellious acts against the Global Community. He's in prison with a life sentence."

Judd shook his head. He told Mac about Pavel's funeral. "You can bet he's leading even more people to faith inside that prison."

"You got that right," Mac said.

"I called because I have a couple questions. The first is about Hattie Durham. Is it true she died in a plane crash?"

Mac sighed. "That was a big GC ruse. We think she's alive. Rayford said Hattie was ticked when she left the States. She's after Carpathia."

"She wants to kill him?"

"Rayford's trying to find her before she blows their cover or gets herself killed."

"Where is she?" Judd said.

"Europe somewhere, we think. Biding her

time until she can get close to the big guy. What else you want to know?"

"We all watched the ceremony with you, Carpathia, and Fortunato."

Mac chuckled. "Yeah, the chance of a lifetime."

"What really happened in Johannesburg?"

"Well, it wasn't like Leon said. To hear him tell it, the GC was on the scene and took care of the assassins immediately."

"If the GC didn't kill them, who did?"

"The horses and riders. We were on our way to a meeting in Africa when my copilot thought he saw horses in the air."

"Did you see them too?"

"I thought he was dreaming or something, but a split second later I saw them. They filled the sky. Abdullah jerked the plane around until we figured out we could go right through them. But Leon and the crew in the back were coughing and sputtering because of the smoke. We landed in Khartoum with two dead and four gasping for air."

"I had no idea the horses could be that high."

"Me either. But we heard an awful lot of Mayday calls from pilots who were going down."

"So you flew from there to Johannesburg?"

"Yeah, Leon was hot to meet with the former head of the United Nations. But when his limo pulled up to the plane, Leon crashed into the cockpit and told us to take off."

"The assassins," Judd said.

"Yeah. I blasted them with some jet exhaust, but they got their guns and caught up. They blew out the tires of the Condor, and we were stuck.

"That's when I noticed there wasn't another plane in sight. No emergency vehicles. Nothing."

"It was a setup."

"Exactly. I didn't think we were going to survive. We had two pistols in the cargo hold, but by then they'd opened up on us and ripped holes in the fuselage. We were pinned down on the floor of the plane."

"How *did* you survive?"

"I got on the radio and called in a Mayday. That's when they threw in the concussion bomb and the plane filled with smoke. We were on fire with nowhere to go. Abdullah and I opened the main cabin door, and we all tumbled out before the fire caught up to us."

"Weren't the assassins waiting for you?" Judd said.

"Tell you the truth, I shut my eyes so tight I thought my cheekbones were in my forehead. I figured I'd open my eyes in heaven.

There was smoke and fire, gunshots, Leon screaming for God to help him . . . I thought we were dead. I fell on top of Leon as we hit the ground, and a bullet ripped open my right shoulder. Another hit my right hand, and I was waiting for a shot to the head.

"Then everything got real still. I thought maybe the gunmen knew they had us and were walking up to finish the job. When I looked up, the smoke was so heavy I could hardly see past my nose. Then I caught sight of them."

"The gunmen?"

"The cavalry," Mac said. "I don't know if you've seen them, but these things were hovering off the ground, galloping and trotting around. They looked even worse than the locusts. They swished their snake tails and snorted fire and smoke. They were only about a hundred feet away. Two of the assassins were near the plane, dead. They had been close enough to kill us all with their next shots. The other one ran down the runway."

"So that's why I saw that little smile on your face when Fortunato said the GC had killed the assassins."

Mac laughed. "I couldn't help it."

"So you saved Fortunato's life?"

"Not on purpose, but it worked out that way."

"Spend much time in the hospital?"

"Yeah, I had some major work done on my shoulder and hand. They saved all the fingers, but I can't do much with them. My thumb won't bend. Best thing that came out of that ordeal is that we met two believers who work with the International Commodity Co-op. A couple from Oklahoma saved our hides with Leon. It's a long story, but a happy ending."

"What happens now?"

"For the next few weeks we'll be off on a tour. The ten regional potentates are supposed to roll out the red carpet for Leon so he can personally invite them to the Gala in September."

Judd thanked Mac for the information and asked his opinion on getting back to the States.

"Travel is still difficult with the plague. There's no telling how long that will last. The GC estimates about 10 percent of the population has died since the start of the smoke and fire and sulfur. That means about three times that will eventually die. If you can find a commercial flight, take it."

※

It took Vicki a few days to recover from their trip. She had lived out of a suitcase for so long that she had a hard time adjusting to her own room. Each morning as she awakened, she thanked God for their travels, the people she had met, and the believers who had been encouraged.

The kids met and decided who would and would not attend the nearest GC satellite school when it opened. Conrad volunteered to scout out the site and the best way to get there from the schoolhouse.

Early one Friday afternoon Mark called for Vicki from the computer room. "I think you'll want to see this."

Vicki looked at the screen. It was a message from the pastor in Arizona.

"It was sent to our address, so I read it. I hope that's okay."

The message read:

> *Dear Vicki, Conrad, and Shelly,*
> *First, I can't thank you enough for the computer. It has really come in handy. I think you'll be pleased to know that your efforts here have paid off. The underground church is growing in Tucson. Many unbelievers who survived the horsemen's rampage have come to us with questions. The young believers you taught were able to clearly explain how to have a relationship with God, and many have become believers. I suspect the other areas you visited*

can say the same. You were truly a gift of
God to us.

The other exciting news concerns Jeff
Williams. He has become a believer!

Vicki gasped and put her hand over her
mouth. For a moment she couldn't read.

"Is he related to Buck?" Mark said.

Vicki nodded and looked at the screen.

> *Jeff stayed away from the church for*
> *a few days, then came back. We had a*
> *great talk. He went home without praying*
> *but knocked on my door at 3 A.M. He*
> *couldn't wait to tell me he had accepted*
> *Christ, and he wanted to be sure he had*
> *done it right. I could tell by the sign on his*
> *forehead that he had.*
>
> *Jeff talked to his father the next day. He's*
> *not a believer yet, but they're both attending*
> *our church, and I have great hopes for Mr.*
> *Williams.*

"I can't wait to tell Buck," Vicki said.

"Better read the last part," Mark said.

> *Jeff has asked that you not tell his brother*
> *any of this. He fears for Buck's life and*
> *thinks any contact with him will somehow*
> *endanger him. Please don't give him this*
> *information.*

The pastor signed off, and Vicki quickly clicked the reply button. *Thank you for letting us know this wonderful news. We're excited about the new addition to the kingdom! We'll be praying for Jeff's father. Let us know if anything in that situation changes, and don't worry about us telling anyone. We'll keep the information to ourselves.*

✳

Judd found Mr. Stein excitedly talking with other witnesses one day and asked what was going on.

Mr. Stein gathered Lionel, Sam, and Judd together. "The Lord spoke to me last night and told me there will be more opportunities for people to become believers in Christ. And God will do it right here in Jerusalem, under the nose of the most evil man on the face of the earth."

"What's the plan?" Lionel said.

"God showed me the faces of people who will come here from every part of the globe. Of course they will be here to celebrate Nicolae Carpathia's Gala, but God will meet them here, and he will use many of the witnesses who have been staying with Yitzhak."

"You mean, you'll just preach in the streets?" Sam said. "Eli and Moishe do that."

"True. But God revealed that something will happen during those events that will cause some to turn to him. When that happens, we will be there and I want you with me."

Lionel looked at Judd. "We've stayed this long, might as well stick it out and see what happens."

"I'm in too," Sam said.

"Let's get Jamal and Kasim in here," Judd said. "I want them to hear this."

Judd went to the family's room in the basement and found Jamal and Lina. "Where's Kasim?"

"Out," Jamal said.

Judd explained Mr. Stein's plan and asked the two to join them.

"No need," Jamal said. "I can assure you, we will stay until the week of the Gala."

Lina looked away. Something didn't feel right. As Judd passed the back door, he noticed Kasim walking in the alley. He held something under his arm. Judd opened the door, and Kasim looked startled.

"Where've you been?" Judd said.

"I didn't know I had to check with you when I went out."

Judd squinted. "I didn't mean anything by it. I just wondered."

"Fine. Now if you'll excuse me." Kasim brushed by Judd and headed downstairs.

Judd called after him. "Mr. Stein has a plan to reach people during the Gala."

Kasim stopped and turned. "Whatever the plan is, I'm sure my family will be pleased to help. Excuse me."

Judd shook his head. Had he said something to offend Kasim and his father? Judd waited a moment, then followed him to the family's room.

"Did you get it?" Jamal said.

Kasim unzipped his jacket and paper rattled. "This is the best they had. It will reach the target from a great distance."

Lina interrupted, clearly upset. "I told you I do not like this. Nada is dead. Now you two want to join her."

"Don't worry," Jamal said. "In the crowd, no one will notice until it is too late."

Judd peeked around the curtain. Jamal inspected something. Judd realized the man was holding a high-powered pistol.

"Perfect. Nicolae Carpathia will pay for the pain he has caused us and the rest of the world."

TEN

Questions

JUDD walked back upstairs, reeling from what he had seen and heard. First Hattie Durham, and now Jamal and Kasim planned to kill Nicolae Carpathia. And who could blame them? After all they had been through, who wouldn't be angry enough to want to kill Nicolae?

Now what do I do? Judd thought.

"Did you find them?" Lionel said when Judd returned.

"They're busy."

Mr. Stein talked more about spreading the gospel during the Gala. Lionel suggested they print pamphlets in different languages. Sam thought of renting a huge hall and holding special meetings.

"Why not speak from one of the Global Community stages?" Mr. Stein said.

Judd laughed.

Mr. Stein stared at him. "I'm serious. If it's

what God wants, perhaps he would make a
way for someone to preach from the enemy's
stage."

"I guess it could happen if God wants it
to," Judd said, "but won't the GC crack down
as soon as you get up there?"

Mr. Stein nodded. "Perhaps. But there
must be a way."

Judd waited for a lull in the conversation.
"I have another question. Would it be wrong
for a believer to kill Nicolae?"

"Whoa," Lionel said. "Where'd you come
up with that?"

"I'm just wondering. The guy's going to be
killed anyway. Is it wrong?"

The kids looked at each other. Lionel
shrugged. "He's supposed to come back to
life, so it's not really going to be murder."

"What?" Sam said. "You mean, like some
kind of vampire?"

"The Bible says the Antichrist will be killed
and then wake up."

Mr. Stein sighed. "I haven't considered
this. God does not permit murder. It is one
of his commandments. But there are certain
circumstances, in warfare for instance, where
God tells his people to kill those who are
against him. I would assume the Antichrist
fits into this."

"Back up," Sam said. "How do you know this is supposed to happen?"

Mr. Stein grabbed a Bible and flipped to the book of Revelation. "In chapter 13 it talks about the beast that is Antichrist." He found the passage and read it aloud.

"'I saw that one of the heads of the beast seemed wounded beyond recovery—but the fatal wound was healed! All the world marveled at this miracle and followed the beast in awe.'"

"So, how's he supposed to be killed?" Sam said. "Does it say?"

"In the following verses it talks about another person who is able to deceive the world. This person requires everyone to worship the one who was wounded. A later verse refers to 'the beast who was fatally wounded and then came back to life.' I take that to mean that Antichrist is to be wounded in the head by a sword. The language there could be figurative, but I believe Tsion Ben-Judah thinks the same, and he hasn't been wrong yet."

"There's one thing for sure," Lionel said. "Whoever does the killing will probably be put to death on the spot."

"And Carpathia will come out looking more of a hero than ever," Sam said.

Judd swallowed hard. Jamal and Kasim were in big trouble. If they went through with their plan, the GC could come after the entire group.

"Why does God even allow somebody like Carpathia to live?" Sam said. "It doesn't make sense."

"God's plan has been in place since the beginning of time," Mr. Stein said. "Satan and his evil angels and all who follow them are merely part of God's divine design. Satan is God's devil, and he only gets away with what God allows him to."

"But if God knew all this bad stuff was going to happen . . ." Sam paused and looked at Mr. Stein. His lip quivered. "God knew my dad wouldn't respond to the message, but he made him anyway. I don't understand."

Mr. Stein put a hand on Sam's shoulder. "And neither do I. How can we understand someone whose wisdom and knowledge are so far above our own? But I do know this. If your father had never existed, neither would you. And you would not have had the opportunity to follow Christ."

Sam nodded. "I'm thankful I came to know God. I guess there are some things I'll never understand."

"Know this," Mr. Stein said. "Satan and his followers will be punished for their evil deeds. But the next few months and years will be very dark for those who believe in the one true God."

Judd looked up as someone walked into the room. It was Kasim.

"So who do you think will actually kill Nicolae?" Lionel said.

Kasim glanced at Judd.

"I would think the person who kills Nicolae will be filled with anger," Mr. Stein said. "He will no doubt be desperate, willing to sacrifice his life for something he feels is right."

"Will the person be insane?" Lionel said.

"Perhaps," Mr. Stein said. "But he may believe it to be the most sane thing he's ever done in his life. He will be desperate but cunning. To get close enough to the potentate to inflict this kind of wound will be an impressive accomplishment."

When they had finished talking among themselves, Kasim came to Judd. "We need to talk."

"Later."

"Tonight."

Over the next few days, Vicki taught Melinda as much as she could about the Bible, prophecy, and what they would experience in the

Great Tribulation. Melinda soaked up the information. She asked good questions and took notes in a small, red notebook she kept with her at all times.

After their studies one afternoon, Vicki took Lenore's baby, Tolan, so Lenore could take a break. Vicki had always loved kids and figured that one day she would get married and have some of her own. She enjoyed baby-sitting, except for the wild kids in the trailer park where she used to live.

As she played with Tolan in front of the schoolhouse, she thought about the kids she used to run with and where they were. Most of them had probably died in one of the plagues.

Shelly brought Tolan's food and sat beside her. Vicki told her what she was thinking, and Shelly nodded. "Sometimes I play the what-if? game. You know, what if the Rapture hadn't happened? What if the Young Trib Force had never gotten together? What if I hadn't become a believer?"

"What are the answers?"

"For all the bad stuff that's happened to the world, I wouldn't change anything because now I know the truth."

Vicki nodded. "I was just thinking about who I might have married if things had stayed like they were."

"Did you have a steady boyfriend?"

"There were a bunch of guys I used to party with. I'm not proud of it, but it's the truth. If I'd stayed mixed up with them, I'd be an alcoholic or in jail or both."

"What about now? Where do you see yourself in a couple of years?"

"I don't know," Vicki said. She took Tolan by both hands and pulled him to a sitting position. "This is probably the most eligible bachelor among us."

"And the cutest," Shelly laughed.

Conrad drove the sports car up the long driveway. Vicki elbowed Shelly. "Did something happen between you and Conrad during the trip?"

"We did have a lot of time to talk." Shelly smiled. "Conrad's a nice guy. He sure cares a lot about you and the others."

Conrad sat down and asked to hold Tolan. Vicki handed the boy to him, and Conrad lay back and put him on his chest. Tolan giggled and tried to grab Conrad's nose.

"He's good with kids too," Vicki whispered.

Shelly rolled her eyes.

"What did you find out about the satellite school?" Vicki said.

Conrad handed Vicki a pamphlet. "Plenty.

First session is a week from today. Kids are actually lining up to register."

Vicki studied the pamphlet. On the front was the insignia of the Global Community. Nicolae Carpathia's face was at the top. Pictures of teenagers from around the world were shown underneath.

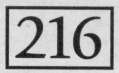

ANNOUNCING THE OPENING OF GLOBAL
COMMUNITY SATELLITE SCHOOL #1134.

The date of the opening sessions was given as well as registration times.

ALL STUDENTS TWENTY YEARS OF AGE AND
YOUNGER MUST SIGN UP. COME PREPARED WITH
AT LEAST TWO PIECES OF IDENTIFICATION.

"Are they fingerprinting?" Shelly said.

Conrad shook his head. "I don't think so. But they were unloading some big machines as I left. One of the workers said a new ID system is in the works."

Vicki felt a chill. "You know what that means. Pretty soon Carpathia will unveil his plans for making everyone take his identification."

"The mark of the beast?" Shelly said.

Vicki nodded and flipped the pamphlet open.

> *The world we see today is very different from the one we knew a few years ago. People of all ages are looking for answers. For young people, this is a stressful time. You've lost family and friends. You want to know what will happen in the future.*
>
> *That's why Potentate Nicolae Carpathia and the leaders in education around the world have teamed to bring you Global Community Satellite Schools. You don't need math and science right now. You don't need tests in English composition. You need to know how to survive.*
>
> *Potentate Carpathia wants every young person to fulfill his or her destiny. He says, "If you want to make a difference for the good of humankind, attend the opening session of the new satellite school in your area. You are the future of the Global Community. We need you."*

The pamphlet gave more specific information about times and locations. "What about the plague of the horsemen?" Vicki said.

"The building they're using used to be some kind of civic center. They're claiming that it's airtight and smokeproof."

"How can they claim that when the smoke even gets into airplanes?" Shelly said.

"They seem pretty confident," Conrad said.

The kids met later to finalize plans on who would attend. Vicki and Darrion already had fake IDs that Zeke Jr. had made for them. They all felt it too risky for Conrad to go, since he had been a Morale Monitor.

"I've decided I'm going," Melinda said.

"What?" Vicki said. "No way."

"I've been praying about it, and I think God wants me to get in the game again."

"You're in the game," Mark said, "but you have to be smart about how you play. The GC wanted you and Felicia dead."

"I know that. But it's been so long, they've probably forgotten about me. If not, I can get a phony ID just like you guys."

Mark shook his head. "I think you'd be more valuable to us here than in some GC prison."

"I appreciate your concern, but—"

"Let's let the group decide," Vicki said.

Everyone voted that Melinda should stay away from the satellite school.

Melinda sighed. "If that's what everybody thinks . . ."

"What's the plan once we're inside?" Darrion said.

"Spread out and see if we can find other believers. Our main job is to figure out the GC's agenda. If we get a chance to share God with somebody, we'll do it. But we have to be careful."

Janie walked in holding one of the GC pamphlets. "Did you guys see this? I want to go."

Vicki looked at the others. "I wouldn't recommend it."

Janie slammed the paper down on a table. "You guys think you know everything. You think Nicolae's the problem. Well, I think he's the answer. And if you're too stubborn—"

Vicki put up a hand. "Janie, you broke out of jail. You're a fugitive. That's why I don't think you should go. The GC will nab you. You don't want that."

Janie looked stunned. "Right. Well, I was going to put on a disguise. I'll do anything to get out of this place."

When Janie left, Mark said, "Maybe Janie going would be the best thing. The GC would catch her, and she becomes their problem."

"I've been praying for that girl ever since I

became a believer," Lenore said. "I'd hate to see anything happen to her."

"How long do you keep praying for somebody?" Vicki said.

The room fell silent. Vicki wondered if there was any chance that Janie would ever believe.

ELEVEN

Kasim's Plan

JUDD was able to avoid Kasim that evening and the next morning, but Kasim cornered him the next night. Judd agreed to talk with him alone in a secluded room downstairs. Kasim's face had healed from the abuse he had taken at the GC jail, but he seemed in pain.

Before Kasim spoke Judd said, "I've been meaning to talk with you about Nada."

"This is not about her—"

"Please. It would help me."

Kasim crossed his legs and sat back. "What do you want to know?"

"We didn't have much contact in the final few weeks. Did she talk about me?"

"We couldn't get her to shut up about you. It was Judd this and Judd that." Kasim looked away. "I hurt her feelings."

"How?"

"She told us some story about the two of you meeting in a garden in New Babylon."

"I remember that."

"She went on and on about her feelings for you. I'd finally had it and said something like, 'Why don't you get married?'"

"Ouch."

"Yeah. I tried to apologize, but she wouldn't talk. My mother said not to bother her. We weren't together again until the GC cornered us."

"What happened?"

"Nada heard something suspicious, and my father went to check it out. We heard the commotion and ran for the fire escape.

"We were on the ground when they burst into the apartment. The squad cars found us with their lights. At the end of the street was a chain-link fence. Nada climbed it, but my pant leg caught at the top." Kasim shook his fists and closed his eyes. "It was such a stupid thing."

"It wasn't your fault."

"She came back to help. I yelled at her to go, but she was determined."

Judd looked at the floor. *That was Nada.*

"If she hadn't come back for me, she probably would have gotten away. And if she had gotten away . . ."

"Don't do this. I blamed myself for what happened, and it almost ate me up."

"Maybe you are to blame," Kasim said softly. "If you had loved my sister the way she loved you, she wouldn't be dead."

Judd stared at Kasim, his heart beating faster. He stood and said, "I'm not taking that."

Kasim grabbed Judd's arm and pulled him down. "Sit!"

Judd leaned close. "I loved your sister. I'd give anything to have her back. I'd take her place if I could. But you have no right to blame me for what happened."

"If you loved her, why didn't you get more serious? That's why she was so hurt by what I said. She knew you would never marry her."

Judd looked away. "Your sister knew me better than I know myself."

Kasim lowered his voice. "I'm sorry. I know you didn't want anything bad to happen to her." Kasim was quiet for a while. He rubbed his arms as if he were cold. Finally, he looked at Judd. "We have to talk about what you heard."

Judd raised an eyebrow.

"Don't play dumb. You saw something or heard something after I came in the other night."

"The GC will kill you if you go through with this."

"Who else knows about our plan?"

"No one. I brought up the question with Mr. Stein and the others. My biggest fear isn't that you'll go through with this. It's that you might succeed, and then the GC will be all over this place and anyone who had anything to do with you."

"The time for fear is past. Now is the time for action."

"Why? You're talking about killing the—"

Kasim put a finger to his lips. "From now on, refer to this as Operation Gala. As to why, I had followed Carpathia as a god. I hung on every word. Now I see how evil he is and where he is leading the world. I don't want anyone to make the same mistake I did. I want to be the one to stop him."

"But you know from reading the Bible that it's not going to last."

Kasim leaned forward. "I don't care. We will do this thing. And whether you like it or not, you are part of our plan."

Judd put up his hands. "No way. If you want—"

Kasim interrupted. "We will leave you and your friends out of it and make sure there is no possible connection, but you must not tell anyone, not even your closest friend. Do you promise?"

"I can't promise that."

Kasim gripped Judd's arm again. "In memory of my sister, for the love you had for her, I beg you to keep our secret. Tell no one."

Judd took a breath and nodded. "All right. I promise."

※

Vicki inspected her photo ID as she waited in line at the satellite school. Her hair had grown since Zeke had dyed it, so Lenore and Shelly helped match the color in the picture. Once again she was Jackie Browne. Vicki wondered about the real Jackie. Who was she and how had she died?

Vicki handed the license to a woman at the front of the line and looked around for her friends. They had parked the car and split up, hoping to meet each other inside.

"Did you register ahead?" the woman said.

"No, I just found out about the school the other day."

The woman shook her head and clicked a computer keyboard. "I need two pieces of ID."

"The license is all I have left," Vicki said.

The woman frowned and handed her a form. "Fill this out and get back in line. I can't promise you'll get inside."

As Conrad had suggested, Vicki gave her address as an apartment building in a nearby town. In the space for the phone number she wrote "doesn't work." She finished and got back in line. After what seemed like days, she made it to the front again and saw a young woman who looked familiar. Her badge said Marjorie Amherst.

"These are the meeting times," Marjorie said. "Make sure you get to the first one. Someone very special is going to speak. If you have any language requirements, you can go to the back of the arena. We have radios for translations in just about any language."

Marjorie handed Vicki a wrist badge that had just come through a special printer. "This is a little warm. You'll need to wear it at all times. You won't be able to get in or out without it."

Finally, Vicki recognized the girl. She had been the valedictorian at Nicolae High when Judd graduated. Judd had said she worshiped Leon Fortunato. Judd had taken her place at the podium when she became too nervous to speak.

"Didn't you go to Nicolae High?" Vicki said.

"Yes, how did you know?"

"I was at your commencement ceremony."

Marjorie put out a hand, and Vicki shook it. "That was such a wonderful meeting until . . . well, you remember what happened."

"Right, that Judd guy got up and ruined everything."

Marjorie leaned forward. "There may be more of his kind around, but don't worry. We'll take care of them."

Vicki winked and smiled. "I'm glad."

Vicki walked through what looked like a huge metal detector. Global Community Morale Monitors stood nearby. Above the machine were two computer screens. The first flashed each person's name as he or she walked through. The second screen scanned each person for weapons.

Vicki wandered through the concrete hallways looking for any sign of Darrion, Mark, or Shelly. She looked for others who had the mark of the true believer as well but didn't find any. Vicki stopped in her tracks when she noticed a small booth set up near a side entrance. The sign above read Tsion Ben-Judah Material.

Vicki shook her head. *Who would be stupid*

enough to fall for that? Since the meeting was about to begin, she went inside to find a seat.

The arena was packed. Some kids threw paper airplanes and even tried bodysurfing through the crowd. Finally, the lights dimmed, and the crowd cheered as the gigantic theater screen flickered to life.

The first image on-screen was a candle flame. A low note sounded and rumbled throughout the darkened arena. As faces from across the country flashed on the screen, a deep-voiced announcer slowly said, "We have come from different places. From different backgrounds. All of us have lost much. Family. Friends. Homes. But we are not without hope."

Nicolae Carpathia's face appeared on the screen, and immediately the crowd rose and applauded. Some whistled. Others screamed. The music rose and drowned out the cheers. The announcer's voice eclipsed the noise. "One man. One mission. To bring peace to all people on earth. He is Potentate Nicolae Carpathia."

Vicki plugged her ears. A girl beside her punched her in the arm and shouted, "Stand up. It's really him!"

Vicki stood. Nicolae walked toward a podium in New Babylon. *Is this live?* she thought. Though he was thousands of miles away, Carpathia seemed to sense the worship. He held up both hands, smiled, then began.

"I greet you in the name of peace," Nicolae said, and again the audience went wild. Carpathia smiled again and raised his hands for quiet. "I welcome participants in this great movement of young people around the globe. In spite of the mysterious deaths we have seen in the last few weeks, you have chosen to gather and learn about the great mission before us.

"Never in the history of the world have we needed our young people more. In the words of a former president of the United States, I charge you to ask not what the Global Community can do for you—ask what you can do for the Global Community."

Again the crowd rose and cheered. The girl beside Vicki turned. "Isn't he great?"

"Yeah," Vicki said.

"If we are to make this world better," Carpathia continued, "if we are to succeed in our pursuit of worldwide peace, we will do so with your help."

The camera pulled in tight to Carpathia's face. The man was handsome; there was no question. He was blond, trim, and looked like a movie star. Vicki remembered what

Buck Williams had said about Carpathia's ability to use mind control. Was he doing this now? And if so, would believers be affected?

As the potentate continued, his face positioned in the middle of the screen, video clips appeared around him. The scenes showed Carpathia holding babies, speaking at the United Nations, walking through cheering crowds, and consulting with other world leaders.

"The Global Community has brought a new ideal to all. Tolerance. We seek to get along with each other, to appreciate differences instead of fight about them. We embrace each other and accept these differences, for in the end they can make us stronger."

The music switched to a minor key, and Carpathia seemed to get more intense. "However, there are those who would oppose our peaceful objectives. People such as the two who inflict plague after deadly plague on the world."

The screen showed Eli and Moishe, the two witnesses at the Wailing Wall. The arena filled with boos and hisses.

"These evil men and those who follow their teaching must be stopped. And I guarantee you, they will be. I will deal with them at the upcoming celebration in Israel. There will be an end to the plagues, drought, famine, and bloody water. When I have dealt with them, we will see the end of rebellion and revolt against the most powerful and loving government that has ever existed."

"So much for tolerance," Vicki muttered.

But no one heard her. The music grew with Nicolae's speech and built to a screaming climax. Kids stood, fists raised in the air.

"I invite you all to join us, either in person or by way of these meetings, for a spectacle unparalleled in human history. The Gala in Jerusalem will be a supreme celebration of peace and tolerance."

Nicolae raised his hands, and the crowd stood as one. Vicki wondered if every arena where this was being seen had done the same.

"I give you my blessing and my full devotion. I will not stop in my quest, for I have been given complete authority. And I now give you this sacred duty. Go into all nations and tell everyone that the true path to peace and understanding lies with the Global Community. Obey what I have told you, and you can be sure I will be with you always. Even unto the end."

TWELVE

The Final Attack

VICKI searched for Darrion, Mark, and Shelly after the morning session. She found them at the prearranged meeting place by a food court.

"Can you believe that guy used the words of Jesus?" Shelly whispered.

"Those are some of the most sacred words to every believer," Mark said. "He twisted them to make it sound like he's god."

"If there was any doubt as to who he really is," Darrion said, "there's no doubt now."

Vicki told them about meeting Marjorie and what she had said about taking care of believers.

"What's she talking about?" Darrion said.

Mark shrugged. His phone rang and he answered. "Hey, Conrad, what's up? . . . You're kidding. When did you notice? . . . I can't believe it. All right, we'll keep our eyes open."

"What is it?" Vicki said.

"Conrad's been up since we left. He says they can't find Melinda."

"Oh no," Vicki said, "you don't think . . ."

"Let's spread out and see if we can find her."

***

Judd and the others heard about the start of the satellite school but didn't dare go near the local gathering at Teddy Kollek Stadium. They tried to find a feed of the broadcast on the Internet but couldn't.

"That must be one of the ways to get people to come," Sam said. "They can't see it any other way."

"They want to get them in the door so they can count how many potential Morale Monitors they can sign up," Lionel said.

Judd felt torn about the situation with Kasim and Jamal. When he saw them, he felt like leaving the room. He had promised not to talk with anyone about their plan, but he felt he had to tell someone.

Lionel, Sam, and Judd helped Yitzhak and Mr. Stein with the daily duties. On any given day there might be as many as twenty witnesses staying in the house or as few as five. Preparing meals, changing beds, and cleaning kept the three busy.

In his spare time, particularly late at night,

Judd searched the Internet for the latest news
and Tsion Ben-Judah's postings. He tried to
keep up to date with what was going on at the
schoolhouse, but the e-mails had been few
since the coming of the horsemen. Judd read
Tsion's latest message, then clicked on the kids'
Web site, www.theunderground-online.com.
Mark had done another good job of taking
Tsion's words and making them understandable for people of any age.

Judd watched the news about travel and
was shocked at how hard it was to find
flights. Smoke and fire and sulfur continued
to affect every aspect of life.

Judd also checked the Global Community
Web site based in New Babylon. Clearly,
many workers had been killed by the latest
plague, and by the looks of the Web site,
many of them were in the technical area.

Though Nicolae Carpathia rarely talked
about anyone but himself, he wasn't afraid
to blame Tsion Ben-Judah for the deaths
around the world. Judd found one newscast
fascinating. Carpathia was in rare form.

There is probably no one more
dangerous on the face of the planet as
this religious zealot, Tsion Ben-Judah.
The man tried to kill me before thou-

sands of witnesses at Teddy Kollek
Stadium in Jerusalem more than a year
ago. He is in league with the two old
radicals who spit their hatred from the
Wailing Wall and boast that they have
poisoned the drinking water. Is it so
much of a stretch to believe that this
cult would wage germ warfare on the
rest of the world? They themselves
clearly have developed some antidote,
because you do not hear of one of them
falling victim. Rather, they have
invented a myth no thinking man or
woman can be expected to swallow.
They would have us believe that our
loved ones and friends are being killed
by roving bands of giant horsemen
riding half horses/half lions, which
breathe fire like dragons. Of course, the
believers, the saints, can see these
monstrous beasts.

Carpathia went on to mock believers and
accuse them of murder.

The Ben-Judah-ites cannot persuade
us with their intolerant, hateful attacks,
so they choose to kill us!

Judd shook his head. Anyone who knew
the truth could see through the man's lies,

but most people followed Carpathia like a god. Judd could see what was coming. If Nicolae said it enough times, he could turn the whole world against believers in Christ. It was hard enough to stay away from the Global Community as it was. What would happen when the Morale Monitors and every citizen kept watch for followers of Christ?

※

Vicki looked for Melinda in front of the arena. The next session was about to begin, but Vicki didn't want to stop.

The hallway cleared as speakers inside boomed with music and voices. A Morale Monitor walked up to Vicki and said, "Can I help you?" Vicki could tell the girl meant, "Why aren't you inside where you belong?"

"I'm looking for a friend of mine. I really wanted her to hear the first session with Nicolae, but—"

"You mean Potentate Carpathia," the girl corrected.

"Right, Potentate Carpathia. Anyway, I don't see her, so I'll head back inside."

"What does your friend look like?"

As Vicki described Melinda, the Morale Monitor inched closer. "What's your friend's name?"

Vicki hesitated. Melinda surely wouldn't have used her own name. But she didn't have a fake ID. "Uh, why? Have you seen someone who looks like her?"

"Come with me," the Morale Monitor said.

Vicki followed a few paces, but when they headed for an identification machine, Vicki ran.

"Stop! In the name of the Global Community, I order you to stop!"

The girl pressed a button on her radio that alerted other Morale Monitors. Vicki ran down the concrete hallway. She reached for a door that led to the arena. Before she could open it, two Morale Monitors burst through.

Mark scanned the crowd, looking for Melinda. There were thousands of faces. He moved to an upper tier and sat next to a boy with binoculars. "Mind if I borrow those for a minute?"

"Sure," the boy said, handing them over. "Did you see Carpathia?"

"Yeah, that was something, wasn't it?"

"The guy that's on right now is their top education man."

"Quiet!" someone in front of them whispered.

Mark scanned the crowd as Dr. Neal Damosa talked about the new world kids were facing. The man paced the stage at a huge arena in Atlanta. His hair was neatly cut, and he wore an expensive suit.

"Probably everyone here and everybody watching by satellite believes that Potentate Carpathia is right when he says there has never been a time in history when we need our young people more."

The audience applauded politely. *Carpathia's a tough act to follow*, Mark thought.

"If *you* don't step up at this critical time, who will? If *you* don't learn to embrace the truths taught by the Global Community and begin to spread them to others, who will? If not *you*, who? If not now, when?"

A murmur spread through the auditorium as Dr. Damosa went into the audience. Kids turned and watched him. Lighting men fumbled, trying to keep a spotlight on him.

"What's this guy doing?" Mark said to the boy beside him.

"I think he's looking for somebody."

Dr. Damosa placed a hand against his earpiece, nodded, and walked a little farther.

"Is there a Stan Barber in this section?" Dr. Damosa put his hand to his ear again and nodded. "Stanley? Are you here, Stanley

Barber? Come out, come out, wherever you are!"

Kids giggled and laughed as Dr. Damosa called the name again and again.

Finally, in another section, a young man of about seventeen stood. He had the unmistakable mark of the believer on his forehead. "I'm Stan Barber."

Dr. Damosa ran forward with a wireless microphone. He asked Stan a few questions, and Stan answered with one- and two-word answers. He was clearly nervous.

"I don't like this," Mark muttered.

"This doctor guy's cool," the boy beside Mark said.

"Stan, let me ask you something. What did you think of Potentate Carpathia's message today?"

Stan took a deep breath. "Well, I suppose it was about like any other message by him."

"Do you think it was good, bad, somewhere in between?"

Stan squirmed. He folded his arms in front of him and looked away from Dr. Damosa.

"You don't want to answer that because you're a follower of Dr. Ben-Judah, aren't you?"

The crowd gasped. Mark closed his eyes and prayed, *God, help this brother get through this situation right now. Give him the right words.*

"The truth is," Dr. Damosa continued, "you hate everything about the Global Community, and you've been working with other teenagers in different areas to fight everything we stand for."

The camera pulled in close to Stan's face. The boy was sweating. Dr. Damosa read Stan's address, gave his phone number and e-mail address, and gave information about the secret church he attended each week. "We've had our eye on you and your friends down here for some time. Nice of you to drop in on our party."

Kids in the audience began to boo.

"Let's keep Stan right here and go to our site near Cleveland. I understand we have someone there who agrees with Stan."

The satellite feed clicked and crackled until a woman appeared with a microphone in front of an equally full arena. "I'm looking for a Deborah Mardy? Deborah?"

One by one believers were called out from different locations. Mark wondered how the GC could have found them all.

"Throw them out!" someone yelled.

"Get rid of the bums!" another said.

The rest of the crowd picked up the chant, and the noise was almost deafening.

Finally, the arena settled when Dr. Damosa came back on camera. "Now, on to a location near Chicago."

Mark stood and looked for the person with the microphone. He saw an older man coming down the steps toward him. No microphone.

His heart beating wildly, Mark looked at the screen. A Morale Monitor was outside the arena. "Dr. D., we have someone here who not only follows the teaching of Tsion Ben-Judah, but is also on the wanted list of the Morale Monitors."

Mark gasped. *Melinda.*

Vicki was nearly knocked down by the Morale Monitors who came through the door. One caught her by the arm and helped her stay on her feet.

"Boy, am I glad you guys are here," Vicki said, out of breath. "That girl over there needs some help."

"Come on!" one boy said to the other.

"Are you sure you're all right?" the other said.

"Yeah, go ahead and see if you can help

her." Vicki rushed into the darkened arena and let her eyes focus. She looked at the screen and couldn't believe her eyes. It was Melinda.

A woman with a microphone was beaming. "We set up a booth and offered free material from the rebel Ben-Judah. When this girl stopped, one of the other Monitors recognized her. She's going to have some explaining to do back at headquarters."

Applause broke out in the arena. Vicki turned to find a seat and was met by three men in uniform.

※

The late spring sun had just set on the horizon over Jerusalem when Judd sat down to write an e-mail to Tsion Ben-Judah. He knew the man was busy and probably didn't have time to write back, but he wanted to explain what had happened in the last few weeks.

Lionel shouted from the back of the house, "Come here, quick!"

Judd ran to the patio and stood next to Sam. Mr. Stein was there with Yitzhak, crowded onto the small space.

Lionel pointed in the direction of some dark clouds. Judd looked closer and realized they weren't clouds. In the glint of the setting

sun were millions of horses and riders.
Smoke and fire swirled in black and yellow
plumes. As they approached the ancient city,
Judd shuddered. The massive horsemen
looked angry and ready for death. The horses
galloped faster and faster, rumbling toward
the city. Their due time had come. All the
other deaths by sulfur and fire were a prelude
to this stampede. The breastplates of the
riders flashed.

"Have mercy on us, oh, God," Mr. Stein
prayed softly. "You have permitted us to see
this cavalry of demons on their final attack.
Let this assault turn many from the evil one
to you. May you be glorified forever."

As Mr. Stein finished, the riders swept past
the patio in a frightening display of power.
Judd rushed to the computer and found the
latest news. Fire and smoke and sulfur envel-
oped the globe. The 200 million horsemen
were loose for a final attack.

ABOUT THE AUTHORS

Jerry B. Jenkins (www.jerryjenkins.com) is the writer of the Left Behind series. He owns the Jerry B. Jenkins Christian Writers Guild, an organization dedicated to mentoring aspiring authors. Former vice president for publishing for the Moody Bible Institute of Chicago, he also served many years as editor of *Moody* magazine and is now Moody's writer-at-large.

His writing has appeared in publications as varied as *Reader's Digest, Parade, Guideposts*, in-flight magazines, and dozens of other periodicals. Jenkins's biographies include books with Billy Graham, Hank Aaron, Bill Gaither, Luis Palau, Walter Payton, Orel Hershiser, and Nolan Ryan, among many others. His books appear regularly on the *New York Times, USA Today, Wall Street Journal,* and *Publishers Weekly* best-seller lists.

Jerry is also the writer of the nationally syndicated sports story comic strip *Gil Thorp*, distributed to newspapers across the United States by Tribune Media Services.

Jerry and his wife, Dianna, live in Colorado and have three grown sons.

Dr. Tim LaHaye (www.timlahaye.com), who conceived the idea of fictionalizing an account of the Rapture and the Tribulation, is a noted author, minister, and nationally recognized speaker on Bible prophecy. He is the founder of both Tim LaHaye Ministries and The PreTrib Research Center. He also recently cofounded the Tim LaHaye School of Prophecy at Liberty University. Presently Dr. LaHaye speaks at many of the major Bible prophecy conferences in the U.S. and Canada, where his current prophecy books are very popular.

Dr. LaHaye holds a doctor of ministry degree from Western Theological Seminary and a doctor of literature degree from Liberty University. For twenty-five years he pastored one of the nation's outstanding churches in San Diego, which grew to three locations. It was during that time that he founded two accredited Christian high schools, a Christian school system of ten schools, and Christian Heritage College.

Dr. LaHaye has written over forty books that have been published in more than thirty languages. He has written books on a wide variety of subjects, such as family life, temperaments, and Bible prophecy. His current fiction works, the Left Behind series, written with Jerry B. Jenkins, continue to appear on the bestseller lists of the Christian Booksellers Association, *Publishers Weekly*, *Wall Street Journal*, *USA Today*, and the *New York Times*.

He is the father of four grown children and grandfather of nine. Snow skiing, waterskiing, motorcycling, golfing, vacationing with family, and jogging are among his leisure activities.

The Future Is Clear

Check out the exciting Left Behind: The Kids series

#1: The Vanishings

#2: Second Chance

#3: Through the Flames

#4: Facing the Future

#5: Nicolae High

#6: The Underground

#7: Busted!

#8: Death Strike

#9: The Search

#10: On the Run

#11: Into the Storm

#12: Earthquake!

#13: The Showdown

#14: Judgment Day

#15: Battling the Commander

#16: Fire from Heaven

#17: Terror in the Stadium

#18: Darkening Skies

#19: Attack of Apollyon

#20: A Dangerous Plan

#21: Secrets of New Babylon

#22: Escape from New Babylon

#23: Horsemen of Terror

BOOKS #24 AND #25 COMING SOON!

Hooked on the exciting
Left Behind: The Kids series?
Then you'll love the dramatic audios!

Listen as the characters come to life in this theatrical
audio that makes the saga of those left behind
even more exciting.

High-tech sound effects, original music,
and professional actors will have you
on the edge of your seat.

Experience the heart-stopping action and
suspense of the end times for yourself!

Three exciting volumes available on CD or cassette.